FRENEMY OF THE
PEOPLE

Praise for *Swans & Klons*

"In the meantime, I'll be sitting here contemplating Nora Olsen's *Swans & Klons*, a YA lesbian sci-fi novel that's one of the best pieces of new fiction I've read in a long time..."
—Noah Berlatsky, *The Atlantic*

Swans & Klons "is a strikingly readable novel with appealing characters and an engaging premise that should keep young readers interested...This is a powerful story, told by sympathetic but not perfect protagonists."—*The Future Fire Reviews*

"It's a high stakes but high spirited adventure, and I recommend it for yourself and the teens in your life."—*Books For Readers*

By the Author

Swans & Klons

Frenemy of the People

Visit us at www.boldstrokesbooks.com

FRENEMY OF THE PEOPLE

by

Nora Olsen

A Division of Bold Strokes Books

2014

FRENEMY OF THE PEOPLE

ISBN 13: 978-1-62639-063-8

This Trade Paperback Original Is Published By
Bold Strokes Books, Inc.
P.O. Box 249
Valley Falls, NY 12185

First Edition: May 2014

Credits
Editor: Ruth Sternglantz
Production Design: Stacia Seaman
Cover Design by Sheri (graphicartist2020@hotmail.com)

Acknowledgments

Heartfelt thanks to:

My late mother, Sondra Spatt Olsen, without whom nothing is possible, and yet here we are. I'm glad you got a chance to read this book in manuscript form.

Lev Olsen, for reading the whole manuscript and giving me wonderful feedback and support.

My old writing group—Kelly Kingman, Cate Fricke, and Jeanne Demers—for your excellent feedback. Kelly, thanks for "helping" me with my back cover copy (i.e., writing it for me).

Maureen Neary, Crystal Malarsky Laffan, and Katrina Charman for giving me such helpful feedback on the opening section of the book.

Juliana Houstoun Potts, for teaching me about horses. Of course, everything that's wrong is my own fault.

Ruth Sternglantz, most terrific editor! This is one case where an exclamation point is needed.

Sandy Lowe and Cindy Cresap, for taking care of, oh, everything. Radclyffe, for being the boss. Sheri, for the awesome cover. And everyone else at Bold Strokes Books.

All the WriMos in the Poughkeepsie region in 2011, especially Jess Streck, L. Josephine Bach, Susan Walsh, Shana Sturtz Brodsky, Rebecca Dingler, Thomas, Maria, Tanya, and everyone else who came to the write-ins. Thanks once again to Chris Baty for inventing NaNoWriMo, and the Office of Letters and Light for transforming ordinary people into writing superheroes.

Nan of Widening Circle blog (dsbutterfly.blogspot.com). I'm sorry I filched your story about greeting every person as if they were Jesus, but I just had to.

Paul O'Hanlon, for explaining what "red line" means, twice.

David Rees and Sam Anderson, for your funny skit about Sassy the horse at the comedy show in Beacon. It was inspiring.

Buddy and Katy Behney, Kendra Wheeler, Doreen Noble, Alex Campone, Harry Manning, Rosie Edreira, James Giordano, Zoe, and everyone else at Bank Square—the best coffee shop in the Hudson Valley and beyond.

Above all, Áine Ní Cheallaigh. I'm so lucky I have the best girlfriend in the world.

To my brother, Lev Olsen

PROLOGUE

Lexie

We didn't meet cute. That's the Hollywood phrase for how a couple meets for the first time in a romantic comedy. You know the kind of thing. He's walking out of the library with a pile of books; she's walking in with a pile of books; they bump into each other and the books go everywhere. You know, cute.

It wasn't like that with me and Clarissa.

We just always hated each other.

Clarissa

Did we even meet at all?

Okay, obviously we must have met for the first time at some point. But I can't remember it. It must have been a long time ago. Probably middle school. My first memory of Lexie is from way back in seventh grade. I remember looking across the classroom at Lexie sticking a wad of gum under her desk and thinking, I really can't stand that girl.

CHAPTER ONE

Clarissa

I should have been worrying about who was going to win the trophy for Best Overall Rider, but instead I was worrying about whether I would be allowed to take home the centerpiece on our table. I hoped my three besties—Jenna, Pacey, and Harney—didn't want it. I didn't want it for myself, but for my sister. The centerpiece was a teal metallic spray depicting a herd of frolicking horses. Tacky, but my sister Desi would absolutely love it.

My parents and my sister usually came to the equestrian team awards banquet, but my parents had claimed they couldn't come because they had some kind of meeting at the bank. A likely story. Who has an important meeting on the Friday of Labor Day weekend? They were probably just sick of showing up at my equestrian events. There were a lot of other empty spaces in the large room scattered with white-clothed tables. Most sports teams hold their awards banquets at the end of the school year, but it's the equestrian team's time-honored custom to have ours just a few days before school begins, so a lot of people don't show up.

We had already gotten through the boring part where

every single member of the team gets a plaque. I really had to pee, but it was time for Best Overall Rider. I knew it was going to be one of us four who would win it. It always was, every year. Jenna won it last year. I could tell Jenna was nervous because she kept fiddling with her long black hair, pulling it back and then dropping it again. I honestly didn't care which one of us won.

Having said that, I did squeal with delight when Mr. Fortescue announced, "Clarissa Kirchendorfer." The team's faculty advisor, who was sitting at our table, congratulated me, and then I ran up to collect my trophy. Jenna had a glassy smile frozen on her face as she applauded.

"This is so great I might pee myself," I said into the microphone. Everyone laughed. The thing about me is I always say whatever comes into my head. My mom raised me to be honest and let the chips fall where they may.

"Everyone here is so talented I almost wish someone else had won, because I would be proud to see any of you win."

I did not say: *Except Jessica Morgenstern, who pushed my sister off the school bus when Jessica and I were in fourth grade, and I'll never ever forgive her.* Even I knew better than to say that. The bus wasn't moving or anything, it was at our stop, but she pushed Desi right down all the steps because she wasn't fast enough, and then she told the bus matron it was an accident.

"Thank you so much for giving me this honor," I said. "I love riding. I love the equestrian team. And now I have to go to the bathroom. Excuse me."

I swept out of the room clutching my trophy. It had a figurine of a rearing stallion, which was silly because that's the last thing you'd want to ride, but I loved it anyway. I won two years ago when I was fourteen, and that trophy was identical except for the date.

It took me a while to find the hotel bathroom. When I got out of the stall, Jenna had joined me in the bathroom. She was polishing my trophy with a paper towel, which I'm not sure was a good idea because it could scratch the cheap metallic finish. I forced myself not to say anything, though—a real effort for me—because I thought she might be disappointed she didn't win.

"The ceremony gets really boring after the Best Overall Rider award," she said. "I thought I'd hang out in here." No congratulations from her. That's not her way.

"Yeah, they should put it at the end, Oscars-style," I said.

Aside from being die-hard members of the equestrian team, the main thing my friends and I had in common was we all had long, straight hair. And we always matched. We couldn't help dressing the same. If I decided to wear a cami, skinny jeans, and ballet flats, when I got to school it would usually turn out the other three were wearing the same. It was like we had a telepathic bond. Right now we all were wearing some variant of a bubble skirt dress, but we had planned that. It made me mad, though, when people at school said we all looked the same. Not true. How could that be, when Jenna and Pacey are Asian, and Harney and I are white?

"There are three other events going on in this conference area," Jenna informed me. "Each one extremely screwy. I can't decide which one is the most depraved."

Jenna is petite and curvy and has a cute heart-shaped face. She's Korean and has dimples. I always want to run my hands through her hair. I only have bangs because I'm copying her. Probably she's the prettiest of us four. Relatively speaking, I'm the DUFF (Designated Ugly Fat Friend) in the group, even though I don't think I'm that bad looking. I'm a brunette and I always have split ends no matter what I do.

We checked our makeup and then made our way back to the awards banquet.

I took notice of the signs outside the other conference rooms, and they were a bit surreal. The Morticians Association of America; Shining Medallion Lesbian Writers Organization; the Ancient Order of Deer Hunters. At the banquet, they were deep into the raffle, which is über boring. My friends and I began to text each other under the table. I could type without looking, but every time the phone vibrated in my hand, I had to check to see what they had to say. Jenna filled everyone in on the odd assortment of groups holding events at the hotel.

Which group is the most depraved? Jenna asked.

Morticians! Harney replied. *EEEWW.*

No the deer hunters. Poor Bambi! Pacey texted.

My dad is a hunter, Harney objected.

I vote the lesbos! Don't let them corner you! Jenna advised.

My big sister Desi is a member of a class of people who is discriminated against; she has Down syndrome. This has made me very sensitive to the issue of prejudice. So I texted, *I don't think lesbians r depraved. I vote morticians.*

Then I was thinking it over, and I decided someone needs to take care of you when you die, so maybe the morticians weren't depraved after all. I was just about to change my vote to deer hunters, when all of our phones buzzed several times in a row.

Our faculty advisor, Señora Modesto, glowered at us. I ignored her because I knew I could get away with it, since she was more like a stuffed doll than a real teacher. She was only our advisor because all school clubs had to have one. But we ran practically everything ourselves. About all Señora Modesto had to do each year was sign the school club form. Even for this event, it was Harney's mom who booked the room and ordered the plaques and stuff. Personally, I thought this venue, the Hilton right off Route 9 in Fishkill, New York, was a bit of a dump, and Harney's mom could have chosen better.

Señora Modesto wouldn't want the centerpiece, would she? But it was just the sort of thing that might appeal to a demented elderly lady.

I checked my phone.

ROTFL, R U a big hairy dyke? Pacey had texted.

The messages from the other two were along the same lines.

What if I was? I said. *R U prejudiced?*

We know U R not gay, Harney said. *Hello, remember Slobberin Robert.*

I dated Slobberin' Robert for two months last year and will never live it down. What's funny is I gave him that nickname just between us four girls, and now the entire school calls him Slobberin' Robert.

Maybe Im bi, I said, not willing to concede the point.

Then, just like that, I realized—Duh! I am so totally bi. Sometimes I get realizations all of a sudden.

I am actually totally bi, I texted them immediately.

It was undeniable once I thought about it. I was drawn to girls exactly the same way I was drawn to guys. I liked pictures of Kimye as much for Kim Kardashian as for Kanye. I had to admit I had probably spent hours thinking about stroking Jenna's hair. And I had sexual fantasies about girls. I didn't think much about it, just quickly put them out of my head and figured it was just a phase. But, like, a phase that had lasted for probably seven years at this point? Let's get real. Was it just a phase that I liked boys?

LOL, Pacey said.

NO IM TOTALLY SERIOUS.

Jenna sucked her teeth, and now Señora Modesto gave her an annoyed look.

U R grossing me out, Harney said. *I am not going bra shopping w you anymore perv girl!*

LOL LOL, Pacey said. Was that all the girl knew how to say? It was ridiculous, because I was sitting two feet away from her and I knew for a fact she was not laughing out loud. Did she not know what out loud meant?

Another realization struck me all of a sudden. I needed some new friends. People who wouldn't run me down. I turned my phone off and slipped it into my purse. I tried to focus on the thank-you speech to our sponsor, Pleasant Ridge Pizza. My so-called friends kept texting furiously. I didn't know if I wanted to spend all my time with them at equestrian club anymore.

The awards ceremony finally wound down.

"Do you mind if I take the centerpiece for Desi?" I asked my friends.

"God, Clarissa, you want everything," Harney said. "The trophy, and the centerpiece too?"

"That's why she's bisexual," Pacey said. "Because she's greedy. She just wants everyone."

I thought they were kidding but I wasn't sure. They didn't usually say stuff like that to me. I decided not to take the centerpiece. But then no one else did either. I glanced back over my shoulder and it was sitting all sad and lonely on the table. Oh well, Desi would never know about it, so she couldn't miss it.

I was getting a ride home with Pacey and her dad. I changed into regular clothes in the bathroom because we were going to stop at the stables. Ordinarily I liked hanging out with Pacey and Mr. Havens because they're so cute. Pacey's adopted, so they don't look alike, but they have the exact same mannerisms. Usually I would tease them about this but today I wasn't feeling it. Mr. Havens drove us in their seven-seat minivan. I don't know if it was awkward or just quiet. We stopped at the barn to visit our horses.

My horse, Sassy, was a chestnut with a white star in the center of her forehead. She made whuffling noises through her nose as she searched me for the apple she knew I had brought her. I took it from the pocket of my hoodie and held it out in my palm, keeping my hand completely flat so she wouldn't mistake my hand for part of the apple and accidentally bite it off. No kidding, horses are cute but they can be dangerous too. Sort of like my so-called friends. I put my face in Sassy's glossy neck. She smelled like horse, but in a nice way. There is a horse smell that has nothing to do with poop.

"You're my best friend, Sassy," I told her.

We groomed our horses, but Mr. Havens was in a rush so we didn't spend long. Then we headed to my house. I live quite close to the stables; in fact, I can even bike over there if there's some reason why I can't use the SUV.

"Do you mind if I leave you at the foot of Bluebird of Happiness Court?" Mr. Havens asked. "I need to hurry home to file a brief." He's a lawyer. They worked around the clock apparently. Pacey told me he took an Ambien once, and then in the middle of the night she found him trying to send a fax with the toaster.

"Sure thing, Mr. H.," I told him. "See you at school on Tuesday, Pacey." I couldn't decide if I was mad at her or not and tried to keep my voice neutral.

She groaned at the mention of school but didn't say anything.

I walked along the driveway of Bluebird of Happiness Court. It's a cul-de-sac, which according to my mom was pronounced *cooled sock*. It's a very new development. Our house was the last one, about three-quarters of the way around the cul-de-sac. More houses were planned, but they were never built. In fact, next to our house is a pile of dirt where they broke ground, then changed their mind, then finally filled it in when it kept filling up with rain water. The whole thing drove my mom crazy. A bulldozer had been sitting there for weeks, spoiling her view of the tiny saplings growing along the driveway. There was a second development planned that never even got started. It was going to be called Owl of Wisdom Court. If you type *Owl of Wisdom Court, Poughquag NY* into Google Maps, it will just show you a bunch of trees.

All the houses on Bluebird of Happiness Court were almost identical, but not quite. They were all large, stately homes, white with black peaked roofs, but other than that there's some variety. For example, our house had steps leading up to the front door, and there's a massive stone arch over the door, with an arch-shaped window cut into it. Only our house had that. And our house was three stories while some of the others were only two. When my parents were looking to buy this house, the Realtor's flyer said it was "a magnificent manor." In my head I always called it the Magnificent Manor. It's way nicer than the dumpy house where we used to live.

"Mom!" I called into the cavernous hallway. Skippy, our golden retriever, bounded up to me, barking, and I rubbed his head. From the living room I could hear the TV. Desi was probably watching *Wendy Wu: Homecoming Warrior* again. She'd been obsessively watching this movie for weeks. It was driving me crazy, but it was better than the Jonas Brothers movies she was watching before.

"I'm in the kitchen, bug," Mom shouted back. *Bug* doesn't sound very good, but it's short for love bug, which she's called me since I was a baby. She used to call my sister Desi *bun* for honeybun until Desi asked her to stop.

The kitchen was my mom's favorite place in the house. She really liked to cook. But I found her on the phone instead of cooking. Practically shouting. A red sauce was bubbling on the stove, so I stirred it.

"I just talked to loss mitigation. They told me to call you, at imminent default. So why are you telling me I have to talk to them? I've been on the phone for—hello? Hello?" She sighed and hung up. "I keep going through the phone tree and getting someone at a call center in India, and then when I finally reach someone who can help me, they hang up on me. It's about the stupid mortgage."

Mortgage was one of those boring grown-up things I didn't even want to understand. Like episiotomy and French drains. When adults started gossiping about those things, I was so gone.

"Oh, thank you, honey, but you should always wash your hands before you start messing with food," my mom said.

"Mom. I'm only touching the spoon. The handle of the spoon."

"Yeah, but you just came from the barn, didn't you? You smell like horse. I don't want any horse in my sauce." She washed her own hands, which had been touching a filthy, contaminated phone, and then began messing around with her sauce.

"Can I tell you something? I'm not sure if I want to do equestrian club this year."

I was pretty sure Mom would be mad about this. My sister Desi had been saying she wanted to join equestrian club. She rides in Special Olympics, and she has a good seat and handles the horse well. But I wasn't sure how the other girls in equestrian would react, and I didn't want to spend all my time running interference for Desi. I figured Mom would think that was why I was dropping equestrian.

To my surprise, she seemed relieved. "That's totally fine, bug. There are so many expenses with equestrian that add up. Why don't you just skip it this year?"

She took that well. "Can I tell you something else?" I asked.

I like to get things off my chest. I don't like having secrets from my parents. And I knew my mom wasn't homophobic even though she's religious. The pastor at our megachurch hated the gays, but Mom didn't. She always said we might not agree with Reverend Stebbins, but we had to respect him.

My mom gestured to go ahead.

"I'm bisexual."

Her brow furrowed. "What does that mean?" she asked. She wasn't kidding. She led a sheltered life.

"That's when you are romantically interested in both boys and girls. Like half-gay, half-straight. You know, like Natalie Portman in *Black Swan*? Only not necessarily crazy or a ballerina."

Mom sighed and stirred her sauce. "Bug, I don't have time for any kind of drama."

"Way to be supportive, Mom."

"Look, just don't tell your sister about this bisexual business. You know how impressionable she is. She'll start saying she's bisexual too."

"What if she is? You always say Desi can be anything she wants to be."

Actually, I didn't think for even a second that my sister was bi. She was boy crazy like nobody's business. And she had never displayed the slightest interest in a girl.

"Come on, Clarissa," Mom said. "Either help me with dinner or step out of my kitchen."

I stepped out of her kitchen.

CHAPTER TWO

Lexie

I hated everyone in school with the red-hot passion of a thousand suns. No one was exempt from my loathing. You know the part in the movie *Clue* where Madeline Kahn talks about flames on the side of her face to describe how much she hates the murder victim? That's how I felt about all these people.

I know how that makes me sound, but if you knew these people, you would despise them also. Don't worry, I'm not a bring-a-gun-to-school type. I just hate silently.

The thing is, they were all completely fake. No one had the slightest interest in anything real. All they cared about was themselves. Even when they were pretending to care about someone else, it was actually really about themselves. They only came alive for stuff like prom, homecoming, sports, making the honor roll, and drinking lots of beer. I'm utterly oblivious to such trivia.

At least my ex-girlfriend Ramone cared about stuff. Like politics, and what's going on in the world. We went to an Occupy Wall Street event in New York City together and slept overnight in the same sleeping bag in a dirty collective house.

Even if it turned out she didn't care about *me* at all, at least she cared about the world and inequality. And she was genuine. Genuine bitch, as it turned out, but not fake. Anyway, Ramone graduated last June, right before we broke up. This fall she was going to Wheaton College. So now it was just me stuck here.

The first day of school was the worst. Because that's when the greatest hypocrisy was on display. That's when they have a special assembly where the different school clubs talk about what they do. Even the ones that seemed at first to be for a good cause, like the environmental club, are actually just about looking good on your college applications.

When I was an ignorant first-year (the nonsexist term for freshman, if you didn't know) I went to a meeting of HELP. I should have known from the name. It stands for Helping Everyone Less Privileged. How can you help *everyone* less privileged? That's a lot of people! When the principal talks about it, he always calls it Helping Others Less Privileged. But that would spell HOLP. Anyway, what HELP or HOLP does is make cheese sandwiches and then take the train into NYC and hand out the sandwiches to homeless people in Grand Central. Sounds good, right? I tried it once. But the people in HOLP were so snotty, both to me and to the homeless people, that it was awful. One homeless woman asked what kind of sandwiches they were, and the leader of HOLP said, "If you're not hungry, you don't have to eat it." Then afterward they were all like, *Ugh I hate cheese sandwiches, let's go to Two Boots and get something to eat. And then let's do a little shopping before we go back. Will you be all right on the train alone, Lexie?* So that was the end of my extracurricular involvement.

I fumed in my spot at the end of the second-to-last bench in the back of the auditorium, as close to the exit as I could get, while HOLP gave their spiel about how rewarding it is to feed the homeless. A sophomore boy was kicking the back of my seat over and over. I yelled at him, but he didn't stop.

Then this girl Clarissa Kirchendorfer got up. That is a classic kind of name these people have. It tells you everything you need to know about her. She was all sunshine and light in a false way, and she was just kind of a Susie Creamcheese type who blurted out inappropriate things. I thought she was there to introduce the equestrian team, which was the activity she and her three clones do.

"Hi there. I'm here to tell you some very special news, which is that Parlington High School has a brand-new club," Clarissa Kirchendorfer said, flipping her brown hair behind her back. "This is the first year for our gay-straight alliance."

My mouth dropped open. Impossible. I had tried to start a GSA last year and I couldn't find a faculty sponsor. I tried all the teachers who I knew were totally gay and in the closet, and they all said they were too busy.

"Our faculty sponsor is Señora Modesto, who very kindly signed the form about five minutes ago," Clarissa chirped, holding up a piece of paper and blowing on the signature. Pure stagecraft because I'm sure it was ballpoint pen.

Señora Modesto was this fossilized Spanish teacher who wore a way-too-black wig that was sometimes on crooked. She'd been here longer than any other teacher. Her class was really easy and kids always took advantage of her. I think she might honestly have early onset Alzheimer's.

I never ever thought of her as a faculty sponsor. Clarissa must be slightly smarter than she looked.

"Now, the name gay-straight alliance implies it's a club for gay and straight students, but actually that's just a name! It's also open to lesbian, bisexual, and transgender students.

I'm not sure what transgender is yet, but I found a website that's going to explain it to me."

I recoiled in horror at her benighted ignorance, bumping into the sleeping sophomore beside me. This was just so wrong. It was like a neo-Nazi student starting a Holocaust studies group.

"So if you are transgender, you should totally come to our group. It's for everybody. Including straight people, right? Like, it has the word straight in the name. It's a safe space for students to talk about being gay or whatever, where there will be no teasing, bullying, or negativity of any kind. So you should totally sign up for the club. All the activities haven't been planned yet, but I think we might do a car wash to raise money and candy grams for Valentine's Day."

Nooo! A GSA was not about candy grams or car washes. This was my worst nightmare, except my unconscious mind could never have imagined anything this weird.

"And if you sign up, don't worry about people teasing you or anything, because remember this club is for everyone. And people should learn to be tolerant and respectful of people who are different. Thank you."

She stepped down. I was so shocked I didn't even hear a word of what the next girl said. I think it was either a film club or possibly something to do with animals.

After the assembly, Clarissa Kirchendorfer accosted me as I was leaving the auditorium. She actually grabbed my shoulder, which I considered an invasion of my personal space.

"Lexie! I hope you're going to join the GSA," she said. She beamed at me expectantly.

Now, look. Everyone in the school knows I'm a lesbian. It was the talk of the school last year when Ramone and I were dating. We never tried to hide it. But it's just rude to go up to someone and out them by telling them they should join the gay club. That is not how some straight girl who decided for unfathomable reasons to start a GSA should behave. She needed sensitivity training already.

"Why do you say that, Clarissa?" I said, staring at her blankly.

"Well, you're the only openly queer person I know of in the school," she said. "That's what you're supposed to say, right? Queer?"

"You have to be queer to get to say queer," I told her. "If you don't understand that, I can't explain it to you."

"Oh, I'm totally queer," she said. "I'm bisexual."

"Making out with another girl in front of your boyfriend to turn him on does not make you bisexual," I told her.

She turned beet red. "I never did anything like that. Who said that? Did Slobberin' Robert say that? Don't believe everything that guy says."

She used to date this guy Slobberin' Robert, who was one of the few people I could tolerate, even though he was a moron.

"No one said it. I'm just saying, just because you're bi-curious does not mean you can start a GSA."

She blinked. "Actually, it does. I called GLSEN and talked to them. Anyone can. Did you know the first student in the whole world ever to start a GSA was straight? All you have to do at Parlington is fill out a form and get a faculty sponsor. I thought you'd be happy about this. GSAs are totally for bi-curious people, anyway. That's *q* for *questioning*. But for your information, I'm not bi-curious. I'm the real thing. Like, I came out to my mom two days ago."

"So what happened to you over the summer? You dated a girl?" I was starting to get interested, despite myself. A lot of girls start out by saying they're bi and ultimately come out as lesbian.

"No. I just realized." She still had a smile on her face, but it looked curdled.

She was a phony after all. "You just realized? How do you really know? Have you ever even kissed a girl?"

The curdled smile vanished. "Look, if you want to sign up for the GSA, there will be no negativity allowed in our meetings. It's a safe space." She turned on her heel.

Whatever. She could keep her safe space. I would rather have my negativity. No way would I join a club run by her.

The one good thing about the awful assembly was we had twenty minutes of free time afterward. The club representatives sat at tables in the cafeteria so you could sign up. The best part was there was free tea and hot chocolate, to lure you down there. I went to get some tea but steered well clear of the club tables. Even though I didn't go near them, I spotted Clarissa Kirchendorfer's distinctive pink-and-white Aeropostale polo shirt. People were clustered in front of other tables, but not hers. She was all alone. No one was signing up for her club.

Chapter Three

Clarissa

What that girl Lexie said really bothered me. I knew she was just being mean-spirited and trying to hurt me, even though I was reaching out to her. She's just like that, all sour and bitter every second for no reason. But what she said was nagging at me, the part about how did I really know I was bi if I hadn't even kissed a girl.

I thought I would like kissing a girl, but what if I was wrong? What if it wasn't like I imagined? Like, I thought I would love the Great American Scream Machine at Six Flags. But actually I hated it and I threw up. In the souvenir picture, which was taken right after the first loop where you go upside down, you can even see the puke starting to come out of my mouth. A thin stream of it. Jenna was so amused, she bought the picture as a keychain even though it was seriously overpriced.

I worried about this the whole drive home after school— the kissing thing, not the puking thing. Although when you think about it, it's the same mouth that you puke with as you kiss with, which is gross. I worried some more when I got home. No one was home, so I could just pace around the house. Then Desi got home—she takes the cheese bus because she does some after-school thing and leaves later than me every day but Friday, when I drive us both home.

"You have to take me to dance class," she reminded me the second she walked in the door. "It's written on my schedule."

"I know, I know. Get your dance bag."

It was Desi's first time taking dance class. She was graduating in June, and Mom was a little freaked out that she wouldn't be able to get a job and she wouldn't have anything to do. So she and Desi planned all these activities that Desi can keep doing after she graduates.

I drove Desi to the nearest Loop stop, which was right outside the Stop & Shop in Beekman. The Loop is the public bus around here. Only people who don't have cars or can't drive take the Loop, so it's all kids, developmentally disabled adults, alcoholics who had their licenses taken away, and some other people who are kind of marginal. In this area, you have to be low income to be carless. We have three cars, but one of them is my dad's classic Daimler, and he won't let anyone use it but him. If he's driving it and it starts to rain, he goes home so it won't get wet. Yet he is constantly washing it. Sometimes he makes no sense.

Desi took the Loop lots of places by herself, but this was her first time going to this dance class, so I had to go with her to make sure she learned her route and wouldn't get lost. While we were waiting for the Loop, a smelly disheveled man staggered up to us.

"Could you ladies spare a dollar?" he asked.

I just looked away and muttered, "No."

But Desi smiled widely at him and said, "I'm sorry I can't help you. But I think you're doing a wonderful thing. Good luck."

The man stopped paying attention to Desi as soon as she said, "I'm sorry," and drifted on to an uptight-looking African

American woman. I vaguely overheard them, but I was staring at Desi.

"Desi," I hissed, "why did you tell that man he was doing a wonderful thing?"

She looked at me, puzzled. "Because he was raising money for UNICEF or another charity."

"No, Des, he was not."

"Yes, he was. That's what people are doing when they ask for money. Like at football games or at church."

Ah. "Sometimes they are. But not this man. He was asking for money so he could buy beer. To get drunk."

She looked seriously shocked. Both her and my mom, and my dad too to some extent, live in this sheltered fantasy world. I could tell she didn't really believe me.

"Or drugs."

"No!" She was so scandalized she didn't believe me.

"Desiree, it's true. So when you're taking the Loop by yourself, or if you're anywhere by yourself, if someone comes up to you and asks for money, don't take your wallet out and— are you listening?—don't start a conversation with them."

"It's rude to just ignore someone," Desi said. "How would you feel if you needed money and everyone pretended you were not there?"

"You can say sorry. But that's it. If they try to start a conversation, do *not* talk to them. This is for your safety. There are some bad people in the world."

Her bottom lip jutted out and she got that stubborn look on her face. "I'm not going to listen to you," she said. "You're wrong. Mom told me to treat everyone I meet as if he was Jesus."

"Oh, for Chrissakes," I said and didn't say anything else to her until the Loop came. Everyone in our family went to church, so I guess we were all pretty religious, but Desi and Mom were, like, extra religious. Someone needed to teach the girl about street safety, though. She clearly had no sense of stranger danger.

I wondered if a creepy predator would zero in on Desi as someone he could take advantage of. Who was I kidding, of course he would. You can tell right away when you look at Desi that she has Down syndrome, because she's petite and has a snubby little nose. Her skin has a softer look, maybe because she has low muscle tone. When she's thinking hard about something, sometimes she lets her mouth hang open a little bit. I don't even know exactly what it is that makes someone look like they have Down syndrome, but I can spot someone who has Down syndrome from fifty feet away with their back turned, just from a glimpse of one ear. When Desi talks, her speech is a bit unclear. We look a lot alike—we both have a dusting of freckles across our noses and arched eyebrows that are darker than our hair, which give us a permanently surprised look. We both have brown hair, but hers is much nicer. Hers is extremely lustrous and shiny and has these streaks of honey color in it, like a shampoo commercial model, whereas mine is lank and plain brown. The highlights I put in myself are not as nice as her natural ones. She has glasses, though, and hearing aids, and I think people see those things first and think she's homely.

"Quit looking at me," Desi said without turning from the window.

"Okay, okay," I said. I stared out the opposite window of the bus, hoping I would get my own car for my birthday this winter. I didn't care if it wasn't anything fancy as long as it wasn't embarrassing. A Toyota Corolla would be totally fine. Desi had taken driver's ed and had passed the written test, and she had been taking driving lessons for a while now. Most people with Down syndrome don't ever get their licenses, but some of them do, and Desi really wanted it.

I realized I wasn't paying attention to where we were. I poked Desi, who was listening to her iPod way too loud.

"Are you paying attention to the stops?"

"Yeah, yeah," she said too loudly because of the music.

"I'm only coming with you this one time," I told her. "You better learn the route."

She waved me off.

I figured she was totally bs-ing me, but what could I do?

Then I started worrying about the kissing thing again.

I poked Desi again. "How do you know you like boys?" I asked her.

She gave me a weird look. "What?"

"How did you know you liked them? Before you ever started dating Bryan, before you ever kissed a boy."

Bryan is her boyfriend. She met him at this disco night for teens with disabilities. At first I thought he was a total loser, but I got used to him.

"I just knew," she told me, looking at me like I was stupid. "I always wanted to kiss a boy. I practiced kissing my Joe Jonas poster."

Luckily it turned out the place where Desi needed to get off the bus was really obvious, and I was sure she'd have no difficulty. The dance studio was in a kind of seedy shopping plaza where half the stores were vacant. I had my doubts about this whole endeavor. We went into the dance studio and introduced ourselves to the teacher. Then Desi went into the locker room to change, and I stepped back outside into the parking lot. I was not going to sit and watch a bunch of grown adults learn modern dance. I'm sure they wouldn't appreciate having an audience either.

I surveyed the small strip of stores. Mom owed me big-time for this. There was a drugstore, a run-down-looking store that seemed to sell balloons and watchbands but it was closed for the day, a Laundromat, and a head shop called Purple Haze.

Then I saw Ramona Hoskins coming out of the head shop. Ramona Hoskins, who went by Ramone, had graduated from Parlington High School last June. She was the only other out lesbian I had ever met. Well, met in the sense of I knew who she was because she was in all the school plays and also mock trial. I'm not sure she knew me. She had dated that awful Lexie. They were both into left-wing things and being strident and frowny, but I got the impression that Ramone was basically a normal person, unlike Lexie.

Here was my chance to get some girl action.

She was heading toward a beat-up Ford Pinto. I had to intercept her before she left.

"Hey! Hey, Ramone!"

I had to sprint across practically the entire parking lot, yelling. By the time I got there, I was winded. She was standing in front of her car with her key in the lock, looking quizzical. She was tall and had a striking pale face, with high cheekbones and dyed red hair. She was holding an unlit cigarette in the other hand.

"You're Ramone Hoskins," I said, panting.

"Uh-huh. I am aware of that," she said coolly.

"I go to Parlington," I told her. "I'm a junior this year."

"Oh," she said.

She wasn't making this easy. Did lesbians have to be unfriendly? What was a good pickup line? I remembered one—*Did your dad have sex with a carrot?*—but that didn't seem like a winner.

"You have beautiful eyes," I told her. Did she? Eh, they

were okay. "Was your father a thief who stole stars from the sky?"

"What?" she said, narrowing her supposedly starlike eyes. She opened the door of her Pinto.

"No! Wait! That was supposed to be a pickup line, but I think I got it wrong," I said hurriedly. "I was just wondering if you'd like to go out with me."

She smiled and looked more pleasant. "That is really sweet, and you are totally adorable, but I'm actually leaving for college in like four hours. My parents are driving me. I should have been there already for orientation, but I had a bad asthma attack. Peter Tosh says marijuana is good for asthma, so I decided to buy some supplies that I don't know if you can get in Norton, Massachusetts."

I didn't understand how inhaling smoke of any kind could be good for asthma, but I put that thought aside.

"Well, maybe I can just give you a kiss then?" I blurted out. "A good-bye kiss?"

She laughed and slammed the car door shut. "Am I even awake?" she asked herself. Then she took three steps over to me and kissed me on the lips.

I knew right away I was totally bisexual.

It felt completely different from kissing Slobberin' Robert. I don't know if it's a boy-girl thing, or if everyone just kisses differently. Her lips were the softest thing I had ever encountered in my life. I felt as if I was having an out-of-body experience; everything was gone except for the kissing. She touched the back of my head and stroked my hair lightly.

Then she released me. "Well, I'll definitely never forget you, whoever you are," she said.

"I hope you like college."

She got in her car, slammed the door, and started it up. The engine coughed twice and then caught. She left the parking lot waving at me. I made buckle-your-seat-belt motions, but she still hadn't done it by the time she was out of sight. I had a big stupid grin on my face. I was a real bisexual, and no mean girl could say I wasn't.

CHAPTER FOUR

Lexie

By the end of the first day of school, I had a plan.

I would apply to Simon's Rock. This was a college about an hour and a half north of here, in Massachusetts, that accepted sixteen- and seventeen-year-olds. It was for people who wanted to go to college early and skip the end of high school.

That would solve all my problems. I could even apply for the next semester. By January, I could be out of my stupid school and my stupid home and in some college dormitory. Perfect.

There were only two potential stumbling blocks. They might not take me because of my spotty grades. Also, my parents might not agree.

My parents wouldn't get home until seven thirty p.m. at the earliest. What can I say, they're hard workers. My mom worked in New York City at a too-big-to-fail investment bank and had a long commute. It kills me that my mom works for one of the most evil companies in America. You can see why I had to be twice as righteous to make up for the stain on my family escutcheon. My father used to work in New York City too, for Goldman Sachs, but then he became an arbitrageur and started his own company. His office was only a few miles away, but he just always worked late.

They worked hard and they also vacationed hard. Three weeks out of the year, they went on exquisite trips. Zip lines in Costa Rica, wine tastings in France, bike tours in Holland. They used to take me until I became too pimply and difficult. When they went away, they would hire Mrs. Álvaz the housekeeper to stay with me. I know this sounds like the clichéd scenario of a poor little rich girl raised by her loving Latina housekeeper, but that's not how it was. Mrs. Álvaz and I have a cordial but distant relationship. She was actually the head of a housekeeping empire and was putting her daughter through Yale, so she didn't have time to get chummy with the customers' kids. Also, don't forget how pimply and difficult I was.

I could not wait to go to college. It was immaterial to me what I would be studying. I wasn't really that into studying. I just wanted to have a great time being difficult, all by myself. The roommate thing could not possibly be as bad as the parents or high school thing.

Mom got home right at seven thirty and juiced herself some carrots and celery in the Breville juicer. I knew better than to greet her until after she drank it. She had to eat really healthy because she was extremely old. She was forty-four years old when I was born, making her now sixty. She was planning to retire in a few years. Still, for her age she was in great shape. A lot of other mothers are these schlubby, comfortable people in sweatpants. My mom was always rail thin, exquisitely tailored, and perfectly poised. Before I was born she had no less than three miscarriages, and so presumably she cherished me very much.

My mom liked me to present her with important information concisely and immediately, the same way she received presentations at work. I had to talk to both my parents in a certain way that, frankly, was not normal. So as soon as she smacked her empty glass down on our Caesarstone counter, I told her, "My first day of school was fine. I have a permission slip for you to sign for a school trip, and I am planning to apply to Simon's Rock, which is a very well-regarded college that accepts only sixteen- and seventeen-year-olds into its freshperson class."

"As a woman who has succeeded in a male-dominated industry, I see no point in these craven euphemisms such as herstory, freshperson, and server instead of waiter or waitress," she said. She had a bit of green on the corner of her mouth. I indicated to my own mouth, and she wiped hers with a paper towel.

"Duly noted," I said.

"This is for next fall you're talking about?"

"No, for the spring semester, starting in January."

"What gave you this idea? When did you come up with this?"

"I went to the guidance office today and asked if there was any way to graduate from high school early. The guidance counselor—counselorette? she was a female—gave me a brochure."

I didn't say that she also told me it was unlikely I would get in.

"So, a well-thought-out plan then. We'll ask your father. It's up to him."

My father came home half an hour later. He had brought a big greasy hamburger for himself, a big greasy veggie burger for me, and lots of fries. He was always very thoughtful about bringing me my favorite treats. Except for me being a vegan now, we liked the same foods. Maybe that's because he truly was biologically my father. I was technically not related genetically to my mom at all. I was the product of my father's sperm and the egg of a woman of the highest pedigree, fertilized in a petri dish and then implanted into my mom. For my money, though, carrying a fetus for nine months and then giving birth to it makes you a mom, and my mom and I did have an authentic relationship. My relationship with my father was always a little more tenuous. I never knew where I was with him. My mom, I got her totally figured out. Love her or hate her, she was very consistent. My dad mystified me.

I set the table with some nice placemats and dishes to eat our greasy burgers off of, because that's one of my mom's pet peeves. My dad tucked into his burger with abandon. He was a big man, and his nicely tailored suits couldn't hide his belly. He was also going quite bald. He was only forty-eight and he was my mom's trophy husband, if you will, but now gone to seed. I didn't really believe in all these superficial judgments about personal appearance, but I knew what they were and that they were important to the world.

"So, Dad, you know how you were telling me to turn my grades around?" I said.

Actually, he just said, "This sucks," when he saw my last report card. But I figured he liked when I implied that he was doing all this great fatherly stuff like encouraging me to do better in school and taking an interest in me.

Actually, who was I kidding? I was the one who liked to pretend all this.

He grunted.

"I am absolutely going to get better grades," I said. "And you know what else? There's this amazing college that takes seventeen-year-olds. If I get in, I can start college in January. Isn't that amazing? I'm going to start working on my application tonight. I could jump-start my whole life and really turn things around."

"High school—best years of your life," he rumbled. He has this deep voice, and I could feel it vibrating through my chest.

"Not *my* life, Dad. I think college will be the best years of my life."

"Then you'll have to pay for it yourself," he said. "I'm not falling for this scheme. You're not going to college until you graduate from high school the normal way. I know you. You'll drop out. Then you'll have no college degree and no real high school diploma either."

"Thanks for considering this," I said. "We'll talk more."

I took my half-eaten veggie burger out to the backyard where I kept a compost pile. Our yard is huge, so I had to walk for what seemed like miles. But the compost was gone. My dad must have told Finbar the gardener to get rid of it. My parents liked to waste as much of everything as possible and use the most planet resources they could, so they hated stuff like recycling and compost.

Disgusted, I tossed the veggie burger over the fence to the neighbor's immaculately groomed yard. I would either hear about this until the end of my days, or I would get away with it. Then I went up to my room and put on really loud music and punched my pillows. I looked in the mirror. My clothes and my spiky blue hair looked tough, but my face looked wan and sad. What a pathetic-looking girl. Even the straight-edge tattoo I had on the back of my hand looked stupid. Usually it made me happy and proud to have a tattoo that proved I was punk rock and vegan, and didn't smoke, drink, or do drugs. But I was too demoralized to be happy and proud.

This fight was not over. This was just round one. I would make my parents agree to this. I hadn't really expected my dad to say yes. Intellectually, I knew I had to be patient. But the rest of me, the nonintellectual part, just wanted to scream and cry.

Now that I was older, I could see my parents weren't really there for me. They were just harsh, uncaring people. It was getting more and more difficult for me to pretend my dad was a great father or that my mother had any feelings at all.

Thinking about my parents wasn't a good road to go down. I needed to think about something else stat. I fired up my computer and went on Facebook. I didn't have a lot of friends in real life or on Facebook, but I liked to see what was going on with my favorite bands and post funny quotations from cult movies and photos of butterflies.

The first thing I saw was a recent status update from Ramone:

After I bought a bong, a beautiful girl in a pink Aeropostale shirt came up to me in the parking lot and asked me out and then KISSED ME PASSIONATELY. I have no idea who she even was!

A girl in a pink Aeropostale shirt.

No…no, it couldn't be. I felt an icy ball of misgiving growing inside me.

I looked at all the comments. Some of Ramone's friends didn't believe her. She responded: *I am not making this up. She had long brown hair and was wearing a pink-striped collared shirt with the Aeropostale logo. She claimed she went to my high school. When I drove away, she made some kind of obscene gesture. For realz.*

God in heaven, it was that skanky abomination, Clarissa Kirchendorfer. What the hell? Was she trying to destroy my life? Kissing my ex-girlfriend just to break me down?

Even though it was as over as could be with me and Ramone, I still felt overpowering waves of jealousy. I had known she would go off to college and get a new girlfriend. But to kiss a random girl in the parking lot and blabber about it on FB? And for that random girl to be insufferable Clarissa Kirchendorfer?

Clarissa Kirchendorfer was my nemesis.

I was going to make her pay—and pay big.

CHAPTER FIVE

Clarissa

I was able to ride the high of kissing my first girl until lunchtime the next day, but the putrid stench of the hot dogs in the cafeteria did me in. Or maybe it was my supposed friends. I was eating lunch with Jenna and a bunch of other girls from equestrian, like I had so many times, but there was something awkward about it. They were talking about dress styles, and they were either excluding me on purpose or by accident. I couldn't tell if I was being too sensitive and overreacting, or if they really wanted to give me the cold shoulder, but I felt very alone.

Then Jenna touched my hand for half a second and said, "I completely understand why you're not doing equestrian this year." I didn't understand her sympathetic tone, and I wasn't sure if it was genuine. Even I didn't completely understand why I had quit equestrian. So what did she mean?

Then I spotted Desi putting her tray down at a table on the other side of the cafeteria, and I felt saved. Before I even knew what I was doing, I stood up.

"Excuse me," I said, "I have to go talk to my sister."

I brought my lunch over to Desi's table. She was having bow ties with red sauce. A total mistake, because the pasta in the cafeteria was always overcooked. The smelly, rubbery hot dogs were actually better.

"There's something really important I want you to help me with," Desi said, without even a hello. She had that shine in her eyes that meant trouble.

"I can't guarantee anything," I said.

"Pleeeease?" wheedled Desi.

"You have to tell me what it is first."

Desi put down her fork and pushed her plate to one side. She said, "I want to be homecoming queen. Like in *Wendy Wu: Homecoming Warrior*."

"You want to learn kung fu too?" I asked. I guess I shouldn't have been surprised. She'd been watching that movie over and over for months.

"No. Just the homecoming queen part."

"Why?" I asked.

"The homecoming court is the royalty of the school," Desi said. "Everyone respects them. I want to make more friends and gain the adoration of the whole school."

"It's kind of a popularity contest," I told her. "Usually some really popular girl is homecoming queen. Most people don't even know you."

"I don't care," Desi said. "I think it's time for a homecoming queen with Down syndrome. And it shouldn't be Shelley Ortiz because she is only fourteen. She's just a baby."

"I don't know if this is such a great idea," I said.

"It's my dream. Mom always says I should follow my dreams."

Yeah, and she also told you that you should treat everyone you meet like Jesus, I thought. I had told Mom she had to talk to Desi about stranger danger, but she had just sighed and said she didn't have time to deal with this right now, and maybe

Dad would do it. Mom seemed to have no time for anything lately.

How could I convince Desi not to do something that would disappoint her?

"Have you thought about who your king would be?" I asked. "It can't be Bryan because he doesn't go to Parlington. Wouldn't he be jealous?"

Desi's brow furrowed. Maybe this would be a deal breaker. It seemed like Desi and Bryan were attached at the hip. Sometimes they had dramatic fights, but they always got back together, usually in a matter of hours.

"Could they make a special exception for him?" Desi asked.

"Absolutely not," I said.

"I don't care," she said. "I'll just have to explain to Bryan that he can't be jealous. This is my last chance. I'm a senior."

I couldn't argue with that. Desi was twenty-one, and special-ed students could go to school until they were twenty-one. This was her last year. Now that I thought about it, a few times recently I had overheard Desi talking to herself and saying something about a queen. But everyone already knew the homecoming king and queen would be Ty Williams and Heather Barrington, the most popular seniors.

"I need your help," Desi said.

"I'll think about it," I said.

She beamed as if I had promised the moon. "Thanks!"

I wasn't trying to be a jerk. But she'd already had such a hard time at Parlington. My mom had to fight with the school every year to make sure Desi could participate in everything. Ever since preschool, Desi did full inclusion, which meant she was in a regular classroom with all typical kids, although she sometimes had an aide or got pulled out for certain subjects.

She basically never saw another person with a disability. Mom always said that Desi could do everything, so she didn't want her in any special programs. But then about two years ago, Desi started coming home crying from school every day and saying she had no friends and people were mean to her. I think she had some friends, but they were getting volunteer credit to be her friend, not like real friends at all. She said she wanted to be around people who were like her, and she was tired of having to be the special one all the time. I thought she was a total drama queen, but Mom was shaken up by it. She signed Desi up for Special Olympics, and also the disco night where she met Bryan. Since then, Desi had stopped complaining about school, but why rock the boat in her senior year?

Desi got up to bus her tray and got in line at the tray carts behind a tall boy dressed in black. I knew he was an arrogant theater dude, and I was pretty sure his name was Hector. After he put his tray on the cart, he deliberately bumped into Desi's tray. Spaghetti sauce splashed up from her plate onto her white blouse. He brushed by her with a sneer. Desi must not have noticed the stains because she just calmly placed her tray in the cart. I wondered if it would be worth it to say something to Hector later or just let it go.

"Hey, you," a girl called to Desi. "Hey, come over here." It was someone at a table full of freshman girls. Desi turned and walked over to the table. She warily kept her distance.

"No, really, come here. We want to be your friends," another girl said.

Desi came a little bit closer.

"What's your name?"

"Desiree Kirchendorfer."

"What??"

"My name is Desiree. Desi, for short."

I was tempted to go over there, but then again, she was

always telling me she didn't want her little sister to fight her battles for her.

"Well, Desi-for-short, we want to be your friends. We love your clothes."

"Thanks," said Desi flatly. I could tell she was on to them, and I was glad.

"Oh no, you know what? Actually, we don't."

"Yeah, because you have tomato sauce all over you. What are you, a pig?"

"You're so bad," hissed another girl. She was giggling, but she looked ashamed too. Another girl was focused on her food and wouldn't look up. I reminded myself these girls had only been in high school for a few days and hardly knew each other. Maybe it was only natural to turn on and try to destroy someone they thought was weaker. Anyway, that's what Ms. Crouch said last period about *Lord of the Flies*.

"You're just being mean," Desi said.

The girls giggled harder.

"It's not funny. I don't know why you want to make me feel bad, but I'm going to ignore you. And you know what else? I'm going to tell the guidance counselor about you. So you're going to get in trouble."

Okay, turn away and leave now, I urged my sister silently. But Desi continued to stand there and stare at them with a look of judgment in her eyes. Like she wanted to crush them with her quiet dignity. Was this part of treating everyone like they were Jesus?

The girls looked worried for about maybe one second. Then the ringleader girl laughed and made an ooga-booga motion with her hands. "Oh, I'm so scared," she said. "Did you hear? We're going to get in *twubble*."

I couldn't take this anymore. I hadn't seen this kind of thing in a while. Abandoning my tray, I walked over to Desi.

I put my arm around her, and she leaned her head against me. She came up to my armpit. I ignored the table of mean girls and acted like I hadn't seen Desi all day, like we hadn't just had lunch together.

"Guess what?" I said. "I am going to help you with your campaign to be homecoming queen. What the hell?"

At that moment my crazy ex-boyfriend Slobberin' Robert walked by. With a flick of his hand he knocked over one of the freshman girls' sodas. Either he had overheard the whole thing and wanted to take his revenge, or he himself was a total jerk. I knew him better than probably anyone else at Parlington, and I didn't have the slightest idea. A brown stream dripped across the whole table and the girls all leaped up, exclaiming and wiping off their jeans.

"Oops," he said nonchalantly and walked away smiling.

CHAPTER SIX

Lexie

All night I had dreamed about Clarissa and Ramone kissing. It made me so furious that my previous anger at Clarissa seemed like nothing more than a tiny ember compared to a raging forest fire.

All day at school I looked for Clarissa's brown ponytail. I thought I saw her a couple times, but it was always some kind of look-alike. I still wasn't sure what I was going to do. Was it better to remain aloof and act like I was above it all? Or maybe just to call her a slut and dunk her head into the water fountain?

Finally, right before the second-to-last period, I saw her in the stairwell, taping up a photocopied sign. She was wearing a pink fitted baby-doll tee with a picture of a cowgirl on a horse and *Yes, I Do Ride Like a Girl* on the back. She actually looked kind of cute, and that pissed me off even more.

"Clarissa Kirchendorfer," I intoned. "Do you know *now* whether you're really bisexual?"

"Yes, I do," said Clarissa perkily. "Thanks for asking. Guess what, Desi is running for homecoming queen. Definitely think about nominating Desi. Nominations will be next week in health class."

I wasn't expecting that response. How can you insult someone who's so thick she's impervious to nuance of every kind? Playing for time, I examined the sign. It showed a photo of a girl with Down syndrome, and it was captioned *Desi for Homecoming Queen.*

"That's a great idea," I said. "I'll vote for Desi. It'll show what a stupid sham the homecoming concept really is if a retarded girl is homecoming queen."

Clarissa's cheerful facade disappeared. Her eyes blazed at me with more emotion than I had ever seen on someone's face in this wretched hive of banality called a school. Her hands balled into fists at her side.

"I have stood a lot of remarks from you, Lexie, because that's how I was raised, but now you've gone too far. Do *not* make disparaging remarks about my sister."

"Your sister?" I said, surprised. But then not surprised. I'd been stuck in the same English class as Clarissa for three years running, and now I could remember that last year Clarissa had read an essay about having a sister with Down syndrome. It was insincere and nauseating, just like the rest of her shtick.

"For your information, Miss Socialist Party-Pants, the word retarded is a slur and you should never, ever say it," Clarissa said.

"Miss Socialist Party-Pants?" I said and laughed. "What—?"

"Not to mention everything you just said is degrading and offensive," Clarissa shouted over me, stabbing her finger in front of my face. With a swirl of ponytail, she stormed off.

"You are overly sensitive *and* crazy *and* a complete phony, *you slag!*" I shouted after her.

"Ooh, catfight," said a random boy passing by. But Clarissa didn't look back, so I continued on my way to class, trying to act casual, but my heart was pounding hard and the blood was singing in my head.

In my incredibly boring precalc class, I tried to sort out how I felt. I had wanted to get back at Clarissa, and I had done it. Was I happy now?

No.

I was having a hard time believing the word *retarded* was offensive. But Clarissa had been offended. And that wasn't exactly how I had meant to get back at her, by insulting her sister. It seemed a bit low. I had only wanted to express my contempt for this overblown popularity contest and the concept of monarchy in high school.

But...

If I was going to be honest, I probably had remembered, on some unconscious level, that Desi was Clarissa's sister. So then I *had* meant to personally offend her. And I had basically said that people with Down syndrome were worthless. That her sister was stupid and a good representative of how stupid high school was. That didn't sound like what I really thought.

While Ms. Cavendish talked about rational and irrational numbers, I surreptitiously took out my smartphone and, in a move I had perfected last year, hid it behind my math book. Without hardly looking at my phone, I Googled *Is the word retarded offensive?*

All the sites that said no sounded kind of intellectually lazy. *It's just a word. It doesn't mean anything. I don't mean anything bad by it.* The ones who said yes sounded more on point. *It hurts people with intellectual disabillities and the people who love them. It's hate speech. It reinforces negative stereotypes.* Apparently *retarded* wasn't even the official word for this disability anymore, so the word existed only as an insult.

It kind of reminded me of the way everyone said, *That's so gay.* My almost-friend Slobberin' Robert said that all the time. He kept saying it was in a completely different context and had nothing to do with actual gay people. Which made no sense. Would he go around saying, *That's so Chinese,* and then not understand why a Chinese kid would get offended?

I was presented with a puzzling ethical dilemma. I hated Clarissa. I wanted to insult her and make her miserable. But I didn't want to be a bigoted person. What was the correct thing to do in this situation?

In my notebook, I drafted the perfect apology. I thought it neither apologized too much nor too little.

Clarissa,

I'm sorry I called your sister that word. I didn't know it was offensive but it turns out you are right. Also every time I think about homecoming or prom, I puke a little and die inside, so it was insulting to say your sister would be a fitting homecoming queen, and I take it back. My wish was to insult you, not your sister, because you are a slatternly strumpet.

I got back on my phone and went on Facebook so I could send Clarissa the message.

But I had pushed my luck too far. Ms. Cavendish came down the aisle unexpectedly and saw me pecking at my phone.

"You know the rules," she said, tearing an infraction sheet off her pad and handing it to me. "No phones in class. Go see the vice principal. Don't come back to my class until you're capable of learning something," she said, leaning in close to my face in a menacing way.

I thought that was a bit unfair. As I walked through the

empty hallway to the vice principal's office, I figured I was learning more than anyone else in the class. I was learning about humanity, and I was willing to humble myself to one of my worst enemies.

There were a lot of other kids waiting for Mr. Viscount, so I returned to my phone while I waited. You weren't supposed to use a phone in the VP's anteroom either, but they had already busted me for it, so why not? I found Clarissa's profile on Facebook. Her profile pic was her standing next to a brown horse. All her posts were about horses too. Obsessed much?

Upon reflection, my apology note could be improved. It lost its martyr-like perfection a little bit at the end when I called Clarissa a slattern. From a feminist perspective, did I really have a right to be so angry at Clarissa for kissing Ramone? Me and Ramone had broken up months ago. Sure, I was mad, that was only natural. But was it really the best idea to act all bitchy?

Also, *slatternly strumpet* was kind of redundant.

In the end, I took out the last sentence, and then sent it.

Immediately, I felt like a million bucks. There was nothing like doing the right thing. My insides were cleansed and pure. When Mr. Viscount called me in and yelled at me, instead of vowing to see him strangled in Ms. Cavendish's entrails, I merely floated above it all on a cloud of righteousness.

"You are not living up to the social contract," Mr. Viscount told me. "If you continue on this path in life, you will be a big failure. It doesn't matter how rich your parents are. Why are you in my office when it's only the second day of school?"

No one can imprison me, I thought. *My soul contains multitudes and flies beyond the choking bonds of this awful place.*

Mr. Viscount let me go in time for the next class. My

phone vibrated on the way, since it hadn't occurred to him to confiscate it. It was a reply from Clarissa, so I ducked into the bathroom to see what she had to say.

It's OK. Thx for ur apology. I appreciate u saying that. Not every1 can admit mistakes & Im glad u lurned something, not 2 B preachy. Im sorry I called you Lenin-Pants or whatev I said. Will you help me with Desi's campaign?

This girl was a whack job. I wrote back:

I don't know if you saw the part where I said every time I think about homecoming, I puke a little and die inside? So, no.

She responded immediately:

Frankly I am desperate. It's OK if u think H.C. is sham as long as u don't say that when u campaign 4 Desi. Ppl are not vy receptive and they just laugh at her campaign so I need help.

I had been railroaded. What could I say? I had to say yes.

CHAPTER SEVEN

Clarissa

After school, I headed straight for the barn. Desi's homecoming queen campaign was causing me so much grief, but I knew riding Sassy and taking care of her would cure me.

I even loved walking inside the barn. The smell of the hay, the light-colored wood of the floor, the sunshine streaming in, all those things cheered me up. Spending time with my horse always took my cares off my shoulders and made me feel like all was right in the world. I liked seeing all the horses peek out to see who was coming. I thought I heard Sassy's distinctive nicker from the other end of the barn.

Mrs. Astin, who owned the barn, was at the rack where the tack was kept, tidying up a tangle of bridles. I greeted her, but she seemed surprised to see me. Then she did a weird thing. She embraced me.

What was going on? True, I was usually at the barn every day, and I'd missed the day before. Still.

"I want you to know you can come visit Sassy anytime," Mrs. Astin said.

I laughed nervously. "I know it's been a couple days," I said. I took Sassy's saddle off its hook.

"But I'm afraid I can't let you ride her," Mrs. Astin said.

"Why not?" I asked. My body jangled with alarm. Was Sassy ill?

"No one said anything to you?" Mrs. Astin said. Now she looked nervous. "Your parents didn't tell you?"

I brushed past Mrs. Astin and ran to Sassy's stall. I envisioned Sassy lying on her side in the straw, foam coming from her mouth. But Sassy was standing there waiting for me, like she always did. Her bright eyes looked inquisitive. She flicked her tail and snorted. I leaned over and blew into my horse's nostrils. That sounds pretty weird, but horses really like it. Sassy made a happy whinnying sound.

Mrs. Astin followed me and put her hand on my shoulder. "Sassy is totally fine," she said. "I didn't mean to scare you. But I do have some bad news for you. Your parents have sold Sassy. You should talk to your parents about this as soon as you can. I really would have expected them to tell you."

I felt knocked off my feet and reached out to touch the stall door for support. It seemed, all of a sudden, as though nothing was real. But I could feel the wood of the stall door beneath my hand, anchoring me in this reality.

"I think there may be a mistake," I suggested.

Mrs. Astin's pitying face was answer enough.

"I'm afraid not. Your mom sold Sassy to me, and I'm going to resell her as soon as I can. I can't let you ride her even though I know you're very safe, just in case anything happened. It's for insurance reasons."

Oh my God, why was she nattering on about insurance? I didn't care about that. That went on the list with French drains. All I cared about right now was my horse.

Why would my mom have done this? I hadn't done anything wrong. I didn't deserve this. I thought back to the last time I had seen Mom, this morning. She had been quiet, still in her bathrobe when she was usually dressed before I even got up. But she hadn't seemed like she was in a vindictive, horse-selling mood. I realized I was clutching one of the posts of the stall door so tightly that my knuckles were white.

"I suggest you go talk to your parents right away," Mrs. Astin said. "And if you ever need a job, I'd be happy to hire you here at the stable."

She left me alone with Sassy then. Probably she expected me to go home.

But I didn't go home. I didn't call my parents either. Instead, I brushed Sassy until I could practically see my face in her side. I carefully combed Sassy's mane and tail. I brought her new bedding and cleaned out her poop even though that was part of the service provided by the stable and Sassy's stall was fairly clean. I picked pebbles out of Sassy's hooves with more care than I ever had before. Then I got an apple from the car, where I kept a whole sack of them for her. While she had her head down, crunching, I kissed the star on her forehead and stroked her ears.

Only when it was dusk and Mrs. Astin flipped on the lights in the barn did I get into the SUV and head for home. My sadness turned to anger during the drive. When I got home, I ignored Skippy's happy greeting and stalked straight into the kitchen. Mom didn't ask me where I'd been. She just looked up guiltily from icing cupcakes.

"Mrs. Astin called two hours ago," she said. "I'm really sorry, bug. I just didn't know how to tell you. There's a plate of chicken Kiev warming for you in the oven."

"How could you do this to me?" I said. "My heart is broken into a thousand little pieces. A million little pieces. If not more! Why did you stab me in the back like this?"

"You said you didn't want to do equestrian anymore, so I thought maybe—"

"Mom. You did not. Buy her back. Call Mrs. A."

"Okay, this is the real truth. We don't have the money to keep a horse anymore. That horse eats a lot."

"Are you kidding?" I shrieked.

"No, I am not kidding. Your dad's business hasn't been going very well, as I'm sure you've noticed."

My dad always had some scheme going, but it seemed like it never worked out the way he hoped. He ran a specialty classic car repair company, for people who had really expensive antique cars that they couldn't trust just anyone to fix. But because of the economy, things had been slow lately, so he had also been doing some regular mechanic work on the side. My mom had her own little Internet business, selling T-shirts and knickknacks that promoted Down syndrome awareness. Stuff like mugs and teddy bears that said *I Love My Nephew With Down Syndrome.*

"I could have helped, if you'd told me," I said. "I could have worked at the stable. Mrs. Astin just said—"

"Clarissa. Listen to me now, because this is serious," Mom said. Her face had gotten all steely. "This is about more than you and your horse. We don't have the money for anything, not just your horse. We might even lose the house."

"I don't care about the house!" I shouted. "I just want my horse!"

I stomped upstairs and slammed the door to my room. Desi did that all the time. Under the circumstances, there was no point in acting mature.

CHAPTER EIGHT

Lexie

It was crazy. For some reason, Clarissa was in front of a soccer goal in my backyard. I was standing with arms akimbo, shouting at Clarissa. I was getting right up in her face. I had no idea what I was shouting. All I knew was that it was good and loud. Clarissa was wearing bright red lipstick, too red to be real. Then I started kissing her. We were rolling around on the ground in front of the soccer goal. It was a perfect communion between our souls, and it felt electric.

I woke up gasping. I didn't even know where I was until everyone started laughing at me. Airless room, chairs, desks, a ring of laughing faces. Einstein poster, Math Squad poster.

Teacher standing over me. Right, I was in precalc.

I wiped a patch of drool from the side of my face. With a grim expression, Ms. Cavendish tore off an infraction sheet from the pad. Her pad was almost used up. There must have been a lot of infractions lately. Not every teacher was as infraction-happy as Frog-Eyes Cavendish. It seemed a little unfair since I hadn't fallen asleep on purpose.

As I waited in the vice principal's anteroom to see Mr. Viscount, I shivered, thinking about my horrible dream. Nightmare, really. No, please, no. Please don't let it be. I had seen that episode of *Buffy The Vampire Slayer*. Not the greatest episode ever, but it looked like it was written by Voltaire compared to some of the terrible episodes in the last season. It was the one where Spike has a dream about kissing Buffy. He wakes up in a cold sweat, realizing he's falling in love with her.

Don't let me be falling for Clarissa. If there is any rhyme or reason in this entire universe, that cannot happen. It would be an abomination, I thought. I would rather fall for bucktoothed, bulging-eyed, menacing Ms. Cavendish than have a crush on Clarissa Kirchendorfer.

I was going to fight this big time. Just because we were the only two girls who liked girls at Parlington did not mean we should get together. That was ridiculous. I had met other gay girls at punk rock shows at ABC No Rio in New York City. I should like one of *those* girls instead.

Mr. Viscount was more subdued today than he had been the day before, but basically he said the same things. He let me go just in time for the next period. But skipping English seemed like a wise decision, since it was the only class I shared with Clarissa. I decided to go to the library and work on my application to Simon's Rock. I got on one of the computers and downloaded it. There was a fifty-dollar application fee that had to be paid by check or money order. My parents wouldn't write me a check, but I knew you could get a money order at the post office, and I had fifty dollars, so that was okay.

At first, everything looked okay. The application had a long list of spaces for extracurricular activities. I didn't think my one outing with HOLP was going to look too impressive. Then I realized I could write about butterflies. I had spent hours learning about butterflies, assisting injured butterflies, and posting butterfly videos on YouTube. Surely that showed both creativity and self-motivation.

But then there was a big problem. Parents not only had to sign the application, they had to write an essay too. An essay about my intellect, relationships, and emotional maturity. How was I going to get around this? My parents had said no to this whole idea. It was probably going to take a while to talk them around. There were only a limited number of vacancies available for the spring semester, and the admissions were rolling, which meant there wasn't a specific deadline. It seemed like it would be a good idea to apply as early as possible. I could imagine tricking my mom into signing the application when she was in a hurry. But an essay? I could not imagine my parents writing a glowing account of me. Ever. Inconceivable. Even if they agreed to let me apply.

I stroked the straight-edge tattoo on my hand and looked at my many rings, trying to imagine what my parents would say about me if they understood who I really was, if they were like other people's parents. What would my mom say? I opened a new document on the computer screen.

I am so proud of Lexie, I typed. *Even though we don't always see eye to eye, I respect that she stands up for what she believes in. When she first became a vegan, I bullied her and tried to sneak meat into her food. But now I see I was wrong, and that she was following her heart. I don't always express it to Lexie, but I really think she is very intelligent.*

I sighed, feeling a liquid glow of contentment. It was great to be appreciated. My mom's essay was going to be amazing. And it distracted me from Clarissa Kirchendorfer. I was probably never going to think about her again.

CHAPTER NINE

Clarissa

I sat paralyzed in front of my computer.

My life was crumbling around me. I had lost my horse, who I now realized was the best thing in my life. I should have appreciated Sassy more. I should have ridden her every single day and been more careful about picking stones out of her hooves. Mrs. A. had said I could come visit anytime, but I was too heartbroken to visit a horse that wasn't mine. Sassy probably missed me and would never understand why I had abandoned her. I just hoped Sassy's new owner would appreciate her and treat her nicely. Hot tears dripped down onto the keyboard of my iMac.

I had also lost my friends, who actually were not very important to me after all. How had I been hanging out with such dud friends for so long? They had known before I did that I'd lost Sassy. And they hadn't done or said anything even a little bit helpful. Jenna could probably cheer me up if she wanted to. She always knew how. But she obviously didn't care. It wasn't so much that I missed my friends, except Jenna a little bit. It was that I had no friends to take their place. I had to eat lunch with Slobberin' Robert. That was okay in a way, but also not okay because it made people think we were going out again.

Then there was Mom saying how we had no more money and we were going to lose the house. I didn't see how you could lose a house, the way you would lose a set of keys or a ChapStick that rolled behind the desk.

Plus I was eating a lot from all the stress, and I was starting to get a big McDonkadonk butt. Now that I wasn't riding anymore, it would only get fatter. I didn't know if my fears about my butt were real or imaginary, and since I had no friends there was no one I could ask. Even our dog Skippy was sick. He was at the vet now, having fragments of a cordless telephone removed from his stomach at great expense. There was nothing I could do about any of this except pray, which I did last thing at night before I went to sleep. Praying in the middle of the day was for total fanatics, in my opinion. So I was trying to forget about it all.

What was troubling me now—to the point where I had completely stalled—was whether or not I should friend Lexie on Facebook. On the screen in front of me was her profile. Her cover photo and her profile picture were both scenes from horror movies. Naturally Lexie couldn't put up something normal. Her profile picture was the girl from the movie *Carrie* with her dress all covered with blood and huge flames behind her. Nice, huh? The girl wasn't kidding about not liking prom.

The only reason I thought I should friend her was that we had been messaging back and forth about Desi's campaign. It seemed weird to be messaging someone on Facebook and not be friends with her, like it was violating an unwritten rule. And I had plenty of other friends who I didn't like that much or I wasn't *really* friends with. But I did draw the line somewhere, and in the past that line had been drawn with

Jessica Morgenstern, the girl who had pushed Desi off the bus seven years ago.

Did I loathe Lexie as much as I hated Jessica Morgenstern? Technically I had forgiven Lexie since she had apologized, something Jessica Morgenstern had never done. And if I despised Lexie so much, why was I getting her to help with the campaign? How, in fact, did it help to get the most sullen, bitter, and unpopular girl in the school to help with the campaign? Lexie was ridiculous—she had a tattoo on her hand that said sXe. She couldn't even spell the word *sex* right. So should I friend her or not?

I had been sitting there frozen in front of the screen for at least five minutes. I fiddled with a blown ostrich egg my uncle had given me—he owned an ostrich farm—that I kept next to my computer. It was enormous, a creamy greenish-yellow color, and very smooth to the touch. I usually found it calming, but it wasn't helping me make a decision about Lexie.

Desi came into my bedroom and sat on the edge of my bed. I hastily brushed the tears from my cheeks. Our parents were out, so it seemed wrong to tell her to get out of my bedroom the way I normally would. Plus, all morning and last night she had been sulking about something Mom and Dad wouldn't let her go to with her boyfriend. She could sulk better than anyone I ever met, and I didn't want to send her back into all that sighing and folded arms and refusing to do everything that wasn't food-related.

"What kind of crown does the homecoming queen wear?" she asked.

"It's not a real crown."

"What do you mean, not real?"

"I mean, it exists, but it's not made of gold and encrusted with diamonds. That would be too heavy anyway. It's a sparkly tiara."

"I don't know what that is."

"I'll show you pictures on the Internet."

Desi came to look over my shoulder. "Eew, who's that?" she asked, pointing at Lexie's page.

"That's Lexie Ganz's profile," I said. "But that's not really a picture of her."

I thought about the scene in *Carrie* where the mother warns Carrie that they're all going to laugh at her at the prom. Okay, the mother is evil, but she's also right. They did all laugh at Carrie. Would everyone laugh at Desi at homecoming? Desi didn't have the ability to set everyone on fire, and she probably wouldn't anyway. That's not how you would treat Jesus, setting him on fire. I really hoped Desi wasn't being set up for a big humiliation. Maybe I should have discouraged her from this whole thing instead of egging her on.

"I know her," Desi said. "She has short blue hair in little spikes, right? She came and talked to me on Thursday while I was waiting for the school bus home. The bus was late again."

"She did? Was she nice?"

I bet she wasn't. I won't friend her, I thought.

"Yeah. She said she would help me be homecoming queen. We talked for a long time. She wanted to know why I wanted to be homecoming queen. She said she needed to understand my motivations."

"So what did you tell her?"

"I said I want to be popular and wear a crown. She said I would be better than Heather Barrington as homecoming queen because I am sincere and Heather is phony. I don't think Heather is phony. Lexie said it's okay if we disagree about that."

I didn't think Heather was phony either. I got along very well with her. Heather always treated Desi, and everyone else, with friendliness. Maybe it was so she could be popular and well-liked, but who cares why as long as she did the right thing? On the other hand, I couldn't picture Heather Barrington engaging Desi in a long conversation about her thoughts and feelings the way Lexie apparently had.

I will friend her, I thought. My mouse hovered over the *Add Friend* button. But then I thought maybe I should show Desi images of tiaras first and put the friending question off a little longer.

Then I heard the distinct sound of the front door shutting and someone walking in downstairs. But no one called out. Everyone in my family shouted out when they entered the house unless something tragic had happened, like their horse being sold.

I glanced at Desi, but she was staring at the screen. Mom and Dad were at an appointment at the bank, and they had said they wouldn't be back until four p.m. Had the appointment gone wrong?

"Mom?" I called out.

No one answered. But there was a sound of footsteps. Heavy footsteps.

"Dad?"

No response. I ran to the window and peeped out. My parents had taken the SUV. And the Beemer was at the shop; it had broken down like it did every few months. But there was a black van parked in the driveway. The intruder must have thought no one was home. Now they had heard me, though.

"Desi, go into my bathroom," I said in a harsh whisper, pulling my startled sister off my bed and shoving her toward my en suite bathroom. I rammed my cordless phone, the one Skippy hadn't eaten, into Desi's hands. "Lock the door and call 9-1-1."

"What?" said Desi, blinking. It often took her a while to process instructions.

I grabbed the phone back and dialed 911, then put it back in Desi's hands. "Talk to them. Tell them there's someone in the house." Desi's eyes widened. "But don't be scared."

I slammed the door on Desi's terrified face. "Lock it. Lock it!" After a moment I heard the little click.

As I crept out of the bedroom and toward the staircase, I hoped it was just Dad in some loaner car and that I would be humiliated. I tried to walk down the stairs silently, but they kept creaking. I had read somewhere that if you step on the sides of the stair instead of in the middle it won't make a sound. But it turned out that wasn't true.

Downstairs I didn't see anyone. Had I imagined it all? Oh God, and Desi was talking to the police right now. But then I heard the sound of cupboards opening in the kitchen. What the hell, was the intruder making himself a bowl of cereal? Then I heard whistling. Cautiously I made my way to the kitchen. I swung the door open but stayed concealed at the side of the door.

When I saw the man in the sport coat, I was so scared I almost peed myself. It was one thing to *think* there was an intruder and to hear strange sounds. It was another to actually see a stranger standing casually in the middle of my kitchen. He was squat and wide, wearing nice but strangely ill-fitting clothing. A digital camera was in his hands and he was snapping pictures. He took detail shots of the cherry cabinets, the countertop, the island. Then he opened another cupboard and began fingering Mom's wedding china that she never used but kept in the front of the cabinet because it looked good in the glass doors. He kept whistling.

Probably the right thing to do was to hide. The police

were on the way. Hopefully. If Desi had talked to them. What was I doing down here anyway? I should be cowering in the bathroom with Desi, explaining things to the police. This guy could be dangerous.

But I found myself getting more and more angry. Who the hell was this guy to walk around my kitchen, acting like he owned the place? My anger was at war with my fear, and I wanted anger to win. It was a strong emotion that could lift me up like a wave bearing a surfer. Fear was like one of the rubber hammers in Wack-A-Mole; it would slam me on the head. I didn't like the fear.

I stepped into the kitchen, feeling strange and exposed, my bare feet cold on the marble floor. I opened my mouth to shout and confront him.

"Excuse me?" was what came out of my mouth in a squeak. Better than nothing.

The man whirled and smiled at me. "Hi, girlie," he said. "I didn't know you were home."

"What are you doing in my house? Get out!" My voice was still quavering.

"Don't worry about it, honey. I'm from the bank." He stepped right past me like I wasn't there and into the living room, leaving a cloying scent of cologne. I followed him. He was taking pictures again.

"No, get the hell out of my house," I insisted. "I'm not kidding. My parents aren't home and I didn't let you in. You're trespassing."

He paid no attention to me, starting for the stairs. Should I pull his sleeve, tackle him?

Just then I heard a car pull up outside and a door slam. A voice shouted, "Police!" The door burst open and a short police officer ran in, pivoting all around with her gun held in two hands. I threw my arms up in the air. I pictured being shot to death in my own living room. The intruder froze on the staircase.

The officer put her gun down and stuck it in the holster. "Gibbons, get out of here," she said to the intruder. A second cop came through the door, also lowering his gun.

"You've got children terrified," the first cop said. She was a petite, light-skinned woman with a hard face and a mass of black hair pinned under her cap. "If I catch you at this again, I'm going to take you in on charges of trespassing and endangerment and whatever else I can think of."

The man in the sport coat trotted down the stairs, his demeanor still casual. He sneered at me as he breezed over to the door.

"You're wasting police resources," the second cop told him. He was a brawny African American man, very tall. Both police officers looked like extras from a movie, one of those buddy cop movies.

I realized I was shaking. "Thank you. Who was that guy?" I asked.

"His name is Gibbons," the man cop said. "We get calls about him all the time. He sneaks into people's homes when they're being foreclosed. Banks hire him to do it. Sometimes he says he's a plumber who's come to fix the sink, sometimes he just walks in. Where are your parents, hon?"

"They're out. They had an appointment at the bank."

The man cop snorted. He was writing something in his book. "I bet he knew that. Are you the one who called?"

"No, that was my sister. Oh my God, Desi. Will you guys come upstairs with me, please, and tell her everything's okay? She must be freaking out."

The woman cop's radio squawked. "You go," she said. "I'll be in the car."

The cop followed me up the stairs. I was embarrassed for

a second to have him in my messy bedroom, but then I figured he was probably used to crack houses and stuff like that.

I could hear Desi crying in the bathroom.

"Des, everything's okay. The cops are here and they chased the man away. Everything's okay now. Let me in."

A pause, and then Desi opened the door. Her face was a mess, covered in tears and snot. I felt like my heart would break. I had seen Desi fake cry and throw a tantrum so often, but I had rarely seen her cry for real. We hugged and rocked back and forth. Then I pulled a tissue from the box I kept on the back of the toilet and handed it to Desi. "Blow," I said, like we were children again.

"You have nothing to worry about," the cop told Desi. I felt reassured too. His voice and easy manner carried security. "That man is gone. And he wasn't dangerous anyway. He is just a nuisance, you understand me?"

Desi nodded.

"He was investigating for the bank, getting pictures of the house, seeing how much everything is worth, and also trying to intimidate your family. But he wasn't going to hurt you. You're safe. You people should lock your doors, though. You leave them open, and someone like that will just pop inside. Now I need one of you to sign this form, says why we were here. Are you eighteen?"

I shook my head. "I'm sixteen. My sister's twenty-one."

The cop pushed back his hat to scratch his head. "Why don't you both sign it for good measure," he said. I handed it to Desi first because she wrote big, and then squeezed my own tiny signature under it.

"That's fine," the man said. "Now, miss, what's your name?"

"Desiree Kirchendorfer."

"That's a mouthful. Now, Desiree, you were very brave, but I want to ask you something. What's your address?"

"Nineteen Bluebird of Happiness Court, Poughquag, New York," Desi recited. If I didn't already know, I would never have understood what she was saying.

"That's a mouthful too. You did a great job on the phone explaining everything. That was good. Gibbons probably won't come back, but if he does, next time you call 9-1-1, try to remember your address. It takes a while to trace the call. Although I guess you guys are probably moving soon. But when you do, learn your address right away."

I felt a chill at the assured way he said we would be moving soon. It seemed like everyone understood what was going on except me. On the heels of that, I was obscurely embarrassed that Desi had forgotten our address. I remembered when we were small, Mom drilled Desi over and over with our old address in case she ever got lost. I hated when Desi didn't put her best foot forward and show how smart she was. This cop would go away thinking she wasn't capable.

"She knows our address," I told the cop. "She probably just got nervous."

"Yes, I was very nervous," Desi echoed.

"I don't doubt it," he said. "You did the right thing calling us, even though that man is nothing but a pest. I just want to coach Desiree here. Are you girls going to be all right until your parents come home?"

We nodded. I thanked him again.

Des and I called Mom and then watched TV under the same blanket until our parents got back. We ended up eating all the snacks in the house.

CHAPTER TEN

Lexie

When I sat next to Desi Kirchendorfer in the cafeteria on Monday, it had nothing to do with the fact that I was *not* falling in love with her sister. I had barely thought of Clarissa all weekend, except to congratulate myself on not thinking about her.

No, I actually sat at that table a lot. In my mind, it was kind of like Switzerland. A lone kingdom of neutrality. You didn't have to talk. No one was rude to each other or snubbed each other at this table. No particular kind of student sat there. It didn't cause comment if a mixture of black, white, Latino, and Asian students sat there, because it was a nonaligned table.

The only people there were Desi and a boy I didn't know, reading a book. The idea of someone reading was sort of intriguing. Then I caught a glimpse of the cover. It was *The Scarlet Letter.* Homework, then. No one would ever read that book for fun. Nothing to get excited about here.

"Hi, Lexie," said Desi. "Do you have any ideas for me about my campaign?"

"Yeah, I think you need to get a few key endorsements. The way a new product will get celebrities to endorse it, you know? I think that will influence other people to want to vote for you. I'm working on a list of people I think you and Clarissa should approach."

"Will you talk to them too?" Desi asked.

"No. That would be counterproductive. I'm the brains behind the operation. Also, I think you should go tell your guidance counselor about it. Get school support. Get all this machinery working for you."

Desi looked puzzled at the reference to machinery but nodded. "I already told her. She's very enthusiastic."

Robert Gelisano, better known as Slobberin' Robert, sat down at the table with his tray. He nodded vaguely to everyone at the table and a long curl of black hair fell into his eye. He tossed it out of the way in a move that would have looked better on a horse. Horse. Clarissa liked horses. No! No thinking about Clarissa, I told myself sternly.

Slobberin' Robert was a bit of an enigma to me. If he turned out to be a serial killer, I couldn't in good conscience say he was the last person I ever would have suspected. Although his scarecrow-like body seemed poorly assembled, he had natural athletic ability and was good at sports, so sporty gym-rat types liked him. He also did a lot of drugs, so he fit in well with the druggy crowd. So far these habits did not interfere with his budding sports career, or with being religious, so he got along well with the God-loving types, who were a small but influential subset of the student body. He wore big plug earrings, so he got along well with other students who wore big plug earrings. And he was half-Dominican and half-Italian, so he straddled racial divisions too. The closest I could come to classifying him was as a class clown with a dark view of life.

"Lexie, how's it hanging?" he asked.

"Heavy, Slobbo, hanging heavy," I said. "In what movie does the main character saw off his own arm?"

"Too easy," he said. "That would be *The Evil Dead.*"

"Oh really?"

He furrowed his brow, now uncertain. "Yes," he said unconvincingly.

"It was *Evil Dead II*," I said.

He hit himself on his forehead. "D'oh!"

What I principally liked about Slobberin' Robert was his immense knowledge of classic movie and TV trivia. What I principally didn't like about him was he seemed to have a fundamental lack of connection to all of humanity, which even my misanthropic self found chilling. Last year he dated Clarissa, so clearly she had been able to penetrate his defenses and—

No. Stop. No thinking about Clarissa. She couldn't penetrate anything.

"I don't understand this game," Desi said.

"You have to think of a movie," Slobberin' Robert said.

"Okay," she said.

"Have you thought of one?" he asked.

"No. Wait, give me a minute."

I chewed my sandwich and didn't think about Clarissa while Desi was picking a movie. Why Clarissa? It made no sense. Surely I could stop this in its tracks.

"Okay, I thought of one," Desi said.

"Now what you have to do is think of a question. No. How do I explain this?" asked Slobberin' Robert. He seemed quite stoned. I wondered what it would be like to be stoned at school. Not that I've ever done drugs, and I hadn't drunk alcohol in over a year, since I became straight edge.

"You want us to guess what movie it is," I said. "So you ask us a question like, in what movie did so and so happen? But don't say the name of the movie."

"Okay," said Desi. "In what movie is about a high school musical?"

"I'll let you field this one," I said.

"*High School Musical*?" asked Slobberin' Robert gravely.

"Oh really?" said Desi.

"Yes."

"So sad. You're wrong. It was *High School Musical 2*."

I cracked up. Everyone broke up laughing, even the guy reading *The Scarlet Letter*. A pleasant warmth permeated my middle. It reminded me of how good it felt to write my mom's essay about me. I liked this feeling of being included with everyone, kidding around casually. I couldn't remember the last time this had happened. Maybe I could have a misfit group of friends—it would be a heartwarming story: the punk rock lesbian, the girl with Down syndrome, the weird guy, and some guy doing his homework.

"Scummy bear?" Slobberin' Robert asked, bringing out a package of gummy bears.

"I'm a vegan," I said. "I can't eat those because they have gelatin in them. Gelatin is made of horses' hooves." Horses. Clarissa. No!

"Not these." He rattled the box at me, and I saw at the top it said, *No Gelatin. Vegan.*

"I love gummy bears," said Desi. She took a handful. I took some, and then Slobberin' Robert offered them to Scarlet Letter, who said, "Thanks, man."

As soon as I tasted them, I realized they had been soaked in vodka. I had known kids used gummy bears as a delivery system for alcohol so they could drink in school. But I hadn't put it together. Probably the vegan gummy bears soaked up the alcohol better so they could become more saturated. I subtly spit them out in my napkin and no one saw.

I wondered if Desi knew she was having alcohol. It could be like a gateway bear for her. I thought about warning her, but then I remembered Clarissa saying Desi was just a regular person and she could do anything. And regular high school students drank, right?

"In what movie is there a terminator?" Slobberin' Robert asked.

"*The Terminator*?"

"No. *Terminator 2*!" Slobberin' Robert said.

"In what movie are there a hundred and one Dalmatians?" I asked.

"*101 Dalmatians*?"

"No. *101 Dalmatians II*!"

"That's wrong!" protested Slobberin' Robert. "That was straight to video. The real movie was called *102 Dalmatians*."

"That's such a stupid name," said Scarlet Letter.

"I know," I said. "Also, *101 Dalmatians* was based on a book by Dodie Smith, and she wrote a perfectly good sequel called *The Starlight Barking*, but they didn't even bother to use it. It's a travesty."

The other three at the table just stared at me, whether in respect, deep puzzlement, or drunkenness I never found out, because just then, my inamorata Clarissa arrived at the table. I had to admit, Clarissa was actually quite good-looking. Nice legs especially. She was wearing her long brown hair down today. And look, her cute little arched eyebrows.

Her eyebrows did not stay cute for long. The little arches squinched together, and her flawless forehead furrowed. "Des, what are you eating?"

"Gummy bears," Desi said defensively. "I'm not on a diet. I can eat whatever I want."

"Yeah, but you cannot eat gummy bears soaked in alcohol!" She batted them out of Desi's hand.

"Keep it down, Clariss. Viscount is here," Slobberin' Robert said. The vice principal liked to patrol the cafeteria.

"I can't believe this," Clarissa said, completely ignoring Slobberin' Robert and turning on me. "I thought you were better than this. How could you do this to my sister? Just so you know, I am *not* going to friend you on Facebook."

"Me? I didn't do anything. They're his bears," I said, completely throwing Slobberin' Robert under the bus.

"I don't expect anything else from him," she said, her blazing eyes locked on mine. It was kind of sexy except she was so angry. "C'mon, Des. Let's go."

"I'm not going with you," Desi said. "I'm staying right here. You are not the boss of me. I can do what I want. Stop trying to ruin my life!"

Completely contradicting what she had said about staying right here, she thundered away from the table. Then she realized she had forgotten her backpack and came back to get it as dramatically as possible. Clarissa sighed and stalked after her.

Viscount cruised by the table, frowning. Slobberin' Robert tucked the gummy bears into the pouch of his hoodie.

"I thought this was supposed to be the calm, no-drama table," commented Scarlet Letter.

No one answered him.

CHAPTER ELEVEN

Clarissa

After school I drove to the stable and asked Mrs. Astin if she would give me a job. It just seemed like if my family was flat broke I should get a job, so I could pay for my own shampoo and clothes. And maybe help out by giving my parents money, if that wouldn't piss them off and I didn't spend all the money on myself. Mrs. Astin said I could start right away mucking out the stables, feeding the horses, and cleaning the paddocks. Later on maybe I could help with lessons. She said I would get eight dollars an hour in cash to start, and after three months she would give me a raise. She told me to use a wheel barrel to clean the stalls, and I managed to keep my mouth shut and not say it was called a wheel*barrow*, not barrel.

There wasn't any good horse-manure-shoveling music on my iPod. Luckily, shoveling horse manure was not as smelly as I had expected. I shoveled it into the wheelbarrow, then rolled it up a ramp and out a door I'd never even noticed before. I kept thinking about my favorite book when I was a kid, *A Little Princess*. In that book, Sara Crewe had been the richest girl in the school until her father died and left her penniless. Then the mean headmistress Miss Minchin made Sara go live in the attic and work as a scullery maid.

I told myself not to be dramatic. Outside the door a Dumpster awaited me. The only problem was the Dumpster was already filled to the brim with poop, so it was hard to dump my load of horse poop inside. I had to tip the wheelbarrow and then spread the poop around with my shovel, like icing a really disgusting cake, so it didn't fall back out at me.

Next on the agenda was an area I had rarely visited. Mrs. Astin had a small petting zoo where kids could have birthday parties. The goats and sheep in the petting zoo had sawdust for their bedding instead of straw, and the sawdust was soaked in pee and much smellier than horse poop. I didn't enjoy this part. But I decided, on the whole, the job was okay. Mrs. Astin was nice, and I was proud I was helping my family with the sweat of my brow. Maybe I could even save a little toward college if only I could stop buying expensive lattes at Starbucks.

The worst part about working at the stables was seeing Sassy. I gave Sassy an apple and talked to her, but it made me feel like a red-hot band had been put around my heart and then tightened until it was close to bursting. I wondered how long it would be before someone bought her, and if they would board her here. What would it be like to watch some other girl take riding lessons on her?

While I was doing the feeding, Jenna was outside in the ring, riding her horse Peaches. Jenna waved at me when I walked by. I waved back. I was glad Jenna was behaving casually, but I couldn't tell if she was being nice or just oblivious.

When I was done, I put everything away and headed for my car. I wondered how smelly I was, so I tried to discreetly smell my own armpit. At that moment Jenna drove by and honked the horn, and I was caught in the act.

As I pulled into the driveway at home, I couldn't help but notice the pile of flyers and postcards dumped on our front steps. I knew they were all from real estate agents, promising they could do a short sale on the house. Whatever that meant. I knew our house was in pre-foreclosure, but I didn't really know what that meant either. I decided to park the SUV in the garage. After that man sneaking around the house, I thought it was safer.

The Beemer was also parked in the garage, but I did a double take when I saw Dad was sitting in it. Why was he sitting in the dark in the car in the garage? I left the door of the garage open to keep it a little brighter. I went over and opened the passenger-side door and slipped into the seat. I breathed in the rich smell of the leather upholstery. "Hi, Daddy."

"Hi, pum'kin," he said. I leaned over and gave him a kiss on his stubbly cheek.

"So, ah, whatcha doin' out here?"

He sighed. "Waiting for you. We need to talk."

"Okay."

"I'm sorry I didn't tell you about the horse, and you had to find out after. And I'm sorry about that man who broke in."

"Not your fault," I said. I was being semisincere. I didn't think the guy who broke in was his fault, but I was pretty mad about Sassy.

"It is my fault. A man is supposed to protect his family. I have three girls to protect, and I didn't do it. Anyway, from here on out I want to tell you everything that's gonna happen before it happens. So you don't have to find out after."

I pictured myself driving home from school one day to find another family living in our house. And Mom saying, "I'm sorry, honey. I didn't know how to tell you. We live in a cardboard box now."

"That's a good idea," I said softly.

"We're going to sell the SUV," he told me. "You're going to have to take the bus to school like your sister."

"Ugh, I hate the bus," I said. "Can I ride my bike?"

"If you want to show up at school all sweaty and gross, be my guest," he said. "And I'm going to trade this car in. If I can get anything for it. It's been repaired so many times, I don't know what it's worth now."

I was wondering how I would get to and from Mrs. A.'s now, but I didn't want to get sidetracked on that. We were falling into a very familiar pattern. I was complaining, and Dad was talking about cars. He could do that all day. I had to switch things up or he wouldn't actually tell me anything.

"Can you just explain this whole thing from the beginning? What's going on?"

What I really wanted to ask him was, *How could you let this happen?* But I couldn't quite get it out. I knew he felt bad enough.

"Our mortgage was originally with our local bank. It was sold to Bank of America, then Countrywide Home Loans, then City Mortgage, Wachovia, Lender Wells Fargo, and finally MegaBank."

"Slow right down," I said. "Explain it to me just like you'd explain it to Desi. What is a mortgage?"

He laughed. "That's when you want to buy a house, but you don't have enough money. Hardly anyone has enough money to pay for the whole thing up front. So people go to their bank and get a mortgage. That's a loan. The bank is lending you money so you can buy a house. And you pay them back over time. A long time. But it's like the bank owns part of your house. That's what they get in return for giving you a loan. So if you can't pay them back, they take the house away from you. That's foreclosure."

I sort of remembered this from Monopoly. You had to flip the property cards over when you mortgaged something, and no one paid you if they landed on it. It was hard for me to apply this knowledge to real life.

"And that's what happened?" I asked.

"Yeah, that's what happened. But I swear to you, pum'kin, I'm only three months late on the payments. I'm pretty sure they shouldn't throw us out over that. Something hinky is going on. The thing is, I'm having some real trouble making the payments. The rate they signed us up for when we bought the house was a teaser rate, $1,559 per month. And I didn't know. I thought it was fixed-rate, but it wasn't."

"You lost me again."

"When I signed the papers, they said I would have to pay $1,559 per month. And I thought it would always be that amount. But in the small print it said that rate would only last for three months, and we didn't realize. It was adjustable, which means they can change it. Now it's $3,600 per month. We had to find all that extra money every month. We did it for a while. But then we didn't anymore."

"That's like a bait and switch," I said. "That's not fair. They tricked you."

"I was supposed to figure it out," Dad said. "But I didn't. I'm a self-made man. I never even passed the Regents in high school. It seemed like such a great deal at the time. And I really wanted to live in this nice house."

Magnificent Manor, I thought.

"It's so much better than that dump we used to live in, right?"

"Yeah."

"The other thing is we refinanced the house. That means when you take out a second mortgage. Like, you say you need thousands of dollars to fix up your house and make it better, and they loan it to you because it's going to make your house worth more money. Only we didn't actually end up using it on fixing up the house. That was right when your sister got her front tooth knocked out in gym class, and we spent some of it on her new tooth. We just used the leftover money on this and that. I gave some money to my brother when he started that ostrich farm. I was a silent partner. We thought for sure ostrich meat was going to be the next big thing. But it wasn't."

I couldn't stand thinking about Uncle Hal and his stupid ostriches. If anyone had asked me, I would've told them it was a dumb idea.

My father cleared his throat. "Anyway, what I really need to tell you is that today we got a letter saying the house is going to be put on the sheriff's sale."

"Wait, what?" I said. That sounded really bad. I pictured the Sheriff of Nottingham, the bad guy from *Robin Hood*. "What is that?"

"That's a public auction," he said.

"They're going to auction off our house to the highest bidder? Like on eBay?" I asked.

"Yup."

"You're kidding." This had to be a practical joke. No way was my father just sitting there telling me that someone else was going to buy our house out from under us.

"I wouldn't kid about this," Dad said, looking down at his hands.

"When?" I asked.

"Next Saturday."

I got cold all over from sheer icy terror. This was a nightmare, right?

"That's so soon!" I said.

"I know. That's why we're having this little chat. I wasn't expecting this either. Your mom's been on the phone all day trying to talk to someone at the bank who can explain this."

"Where are we going to live?"

"Hal says he's always got room for us on the farm. But I hope it won't come to that. We're still trying to work out a deal with the bank."

Someone knocked on the car window and I jumped. It was Bryan, Desi's boyfriend. He was wearing a T-shirt with The Rock on it, which didn't surprise me because he was obsessed with wrestling. He liked to do bodybuilder poses, but he never actually flexed his muscles, so the effect was marred.

I rolled down the window. "Hi, Bryan," my father said. "Did your mom just drop you off?"

"Uh, yes, she did. Uh, Desi and I are watching *Lord of the Rings* tonight. Are you going to watch with us?"

"Not my kind of movie," I answered automatically, still thinking about the sheriff's sale. "I can't keep all those hobbits or orcs or whatever they are straight."

"I'll probably watch with you," Dad said. He didn't like that kind of movie either, but he liked to chaperone them. "Desi isn't back from her driving lesson yet. You want to get yourself a Pepsi or something and wait for her? And Skippy's home from the vet. He's all better and I bet he'll be happy to see you."

"Thanks," Bryan said. He made some kind of weird wrestling symbol with his hands and headed for the door to the house.

Bryan was kind of goofy like that, and I used to think he wasn't good enough for Desi. He was two years older and a greeter at Walmart. He talked the customers' ears off, telling them all about wrestling if they let him. I guess at first I was kind of a snob and thought that wasn't a great job, even for someone with Down syndrome. Plus I thought he wasn't as smart as Desi, and I didn't like how he sometimes started arguments with her. But I've mellowed out and gotten pretty fond of him. He's always at our house and went skiing with us, so I'd had time to get used to him. Desi was like the princess of my family, so maybe I would never think any guy was good enough for her. The main thing was that Desi loved him. If Desi had to leave Bryan to live in Arizona, she was going to wig out beyond belief.

Just then, Desi and her driving instructor Mr. Metzger pulled into the driveway. They were in the Metzgermobile, a tanky-looking blue car with a sign on the top that says METZGER AUTO-DRIVING SCHOOL and, crucially, a second set of brakes on the passenger side. Mr. Metzger was driving and Desi looked all red and blotchy, two bad signs.

"Uh-oh," Dad muttered. "Today they were going to work on changing lanes. I better go see how that went."

He left me alone in the car. I tried to absorb the news he had given me about losing the house. Losing the house this weekend.

My whole world was completely falling apart. Desi said that very phrase all the time, about any old thing, and I knew I had been guilty of saying it about minor problems too. But this time it was real. I thought losing Sassy was the worst thing that could happen. But having to go and live with Uncle Hal?

"Thanks a lot, Dad, for giving me so much notice," I muttered. My parents had obviously known that this could happen for a really long time, and they never told me. What the hell were they doing to fix this? Nothing.

I was not going to move to Arizona and live on an ostrich farm. That was for damn sure. It was called a farm, but Uncle Hal lived in a double-wide trailer, and the ostriches lived outside. I was not going to live there.

If my parents weren't going to take care of things the proper way, I was going to have to do it myself.

CHAPTER TWELVE

Lexie

I had devoted an entire week to not falling in love with Clarissa. Between that and finally finishing my mom's essay for Simon's Rock, I'd kept busy. Both projects were going great. With Clarissa, initially I had tried to focus on how annoying she was and how she was just no damn good. That hadn't worked well. My brain was softening up toward Clarissa in some way. So I turned to the same person I always turned to in times of trouble, a man who had been dead for two thousand years. No, not Jesus. It was the poet Ovid.

Ovid had been a consolation to me during my breakup with Ramone. We had argued over something completely stupid, whether life was better or worse before the invention of agriculture. I mean, a) who knows and b) who cares? But I took the position it had been a golden age when people spent less time procuring food and had fewer diseases. Before I knew it, Ramone was calling me willfully ignorant and stubborn and had thrown her necklace, which I had bought her at the Dutchess County Fair just two weeks earlier, at me and stormed out.

I was too dumb to realize that Ramone was just tired of going out with me and had picked this flimsy pretext to break up. So I spent the next couple weeks locked in my room, trolling the Internet, or in the Adriance branch of the library, reading books on agriculture versus primitive times. I thought if I explained my point of view really clearly with a lot of supporting evidence then Ramone would reconcile with me. Then I heard she had been seen around with a girl who went to Vassar. The only thing that consoled me was a poem by Ovid that said, in part:

Earth offered better things then, rich harvests
    without ploughing,
fruit, and honey discovered in the hollow oak.
No one ever ripped the soil with the plough.
Against yourself, human nature, you have turned your cleverness
    And ingeniously injured yourself.

I had felt totally vindicated. This guy from ancient times agreed with me about agriculture. Plus, talk about turning my cleverness against myself and injuring myself, that was my MO big-time.

Now, like a BFF, Ovid was there for me again when I needed him. In his *Remedia Amoris*—Love's Remedy—he made several helpful recommendations: to stay busy, focus on your beloved's physical flaws, avoid poetry that idealized the concept of love, and duh, avoid the person. So I listened to Coil's cover of "Bang Bang (My Baby Shot Me Down)" and "Either You Don't Love Me or I Don't Love You" by The Magnetic Fields. I also took cold showers. Ovid didn't recommend that, but they probably hadn't invented hot showers yet, or maybe even showers, so he wouldn't have known.

Ovid's last suggestion, avoiding the person, worked okay at first. The only class we had together was English. She sat behind me and she mostly was pretty quiet, except one time when we were reading an excerpt from *The Cherry Orchard*, a play by Chekhov. It was about this aristocratic family whose estate was going to be auctioned off because they couldn't pay the mortgage, and they didn't even try to do anything about it. Everyone was saying what a bunch of stupid losers the family was, and Clarissa went all postal and argued with everyone. Other than that, total silence, and I could pretend she wasn't even there.

Avoiding her didn't work well the next Monday when I had to meet Clarissa and Desi after school for a strategy meeting. Especially when it turned out Desi wasn't there.

"She's home sick," Clarissa explained. "She's got a cold. I hope I don't get it."

"Oh," I said. No chaperone.

"I have a proposition for you, though," Clarissa said.

I focused on Clarissa's stupid bangs. They had grown too long and she was trying to tuck them behind her ears, but they kept popping out and hanging in her eyes. This happened over and over. I had zeroed in on this as her most unattractive physical flaw.

"I know you said you don't want to join the GSA," Clarissa said. "But I figured we could call this a meeting of the GSA, and then say our project is Desi's campaign. Because I posted that the GSA meets at this time on Mondays, and someday a student might actually want to join the GSA, so I have to sit here anyway in case they come. It would be good if I could multitask."

"Whatever," I said. We were sitting in a typical Parlington classroom: cinderblock walls, chairs with little desks attached, depressing lighting set into speckled square ceiling tiles, and anti-inspiring posters on the wall. This setting made me want to throw up and then die. I didn't know why I was even involved in the Desi campaign. I had been trying to avoid Clarissa, and now everything was spiraling out of control.

"I've been working on your list of influential students whose endorsements we need," Clarissa said. "You really did pick the most key people. I never would have thought of Arnetta Johnson, but actually she's like the lynchpin of the Christian students, and if she votes Desi, that's probably fifteen others voting Desi. She said she would do it. I don't know how you can have such a breadth of knowledge about the social structure of this school and yet not…Um. You know."

"Have any friends? Just because I *know* doesn't mean I care."

Clarissa rolled her eyes just a tiny little bit. "Anyway, so far it looks pretty good. The real problem is Heather."

"I figured as much," I said.

"She told me she's been working toward this since she was ten years old, and she's not going to give up her chance at the crown for a Jenny-come-lately. She thinks Desi is well-intentioned but misguided."

"That is bad news. If she's willing to take this to the mat, she can probably get half the class at least. All the Christians and greasy grinds in all the world can't help us."

"Yeah." Clarissa sighed. "I'd really like for this to go right for Desi."

I noticed the dark circles under Clarissa's eyes had gotten worse, and she looked beaten down in general. "Are you coming down with something, the cold Desi's got?" I asked. "You don't look so good."

"Thanks a lot," Clarissa said. She pulled out a little compact and started eyeing herself in the mirror.

"No, I just…I just meant you don't look well. You look, uh, fine otherwise." Actually she looked very fine otherwise. She had just the right amount of junk in the trunk, and oh, those legs got me every time. But she did look ill or tired or something. "Are you okay?" I asked.

"I'm not okay, thank you for asking," Clarissa said, applying some powdery substance to her face with a tiny thing that looked like a sponge.

"Is there anything I can help with?" I found myself asking.

Clarissa put down her makeup and eyed me suspiciously. "You haven't heard anything?"

"Who would tell me anything?" I asked.

"Slobberin' Robert, for one. I wonder if he knows. I know you hang out with him sometimes." It sounded like an accusation.

"We just talk about movies. Sometimes TV."

Clarissa sighed again, and I could tell she was going to spill it.

"Our house is getting foreclosed on. It's really stressful. We got a letter saying the house was going to be put on the sheriff's sale on Saturday, so we packed our stuff into boxes. I went to four different liquor stores to get cardboard boxes. But then the auction never happened. It's like they're just trying to drive us crazy. Even though we're packing, my parents are still trying to work things out so maybe we won't have to move after all. These short sale real estate agents keep ringing our bell like every five seconds. And I don't know where any of my stuff is, 'cause I packed it all. If we do move, it's not like we even have a place to move to. My dad wants to move to Arizona and live with his brother and a hundred ostriches in a trailer."

That sounded like one crowded trailer.

"Jesus," I said. "That is bad. I'm sorry." I always thought a girl like Clarissa would have a perfect life. I guess you never knew what other people were going through.

"Thanks, I guess," Clarissa said.

"Can you fight the bank?" I said.

"They won't hardly answer my parents' calls. What did you have in mind, a protest?" She laughed.

"I know sometimes the foreclosures are fraudulent," I said. "Sometimes if it goes to court, the judge throws it out."

"Really?" said Clarissa. "How do you know?"

"Can I trust you not to tell?" I asked. Why was I even asking? I just shouldn't tell her. How did telling her my shameful secrets fit with avoiding her?

"If you don't tell my stuff, I won't tell your stuff," Clarissa said.

"I know because my evil parents work in banking, and my father made a ton of money at Goldman Sachs betting against their own CDOs. That's collateralized debt obligations."

"Like, I have no idea what you're saying," Clarissa said.

"So this company he worked for, Goldman Sachs, bought these bad mortgages that people couldn't pay, probably like your family's. But they were bundled together into these packages called CDOs. Then they were selling these CDOs to their customers, telling them that they should totally invest in this great opportunity. Even though they actually knew all the time that the mortgages were doomed."

"Your dad did that?"

"No, worse. He worked in a different area of the company. They basically bet on whether things are going to go up or down. My dad bet a lot of money that the mortgages were bad and would default. He made a ton of money for Goldman Sachs. They gave him more than a million dollars in bonuses, they were so happy with him."

I wasn't even sure why I was telling Clarissa all this. These were my deepest, darkest secrets. For some reason, against all my better judgment, I thought I could trust her.

"And they never got mad at him later?"

"No," I said. "But he doesn't work there any more. He went

out on his own. He started a hedge fund. He's an arbitrageur. Don't tell anyone, okay?"

"You don't want people to know how rich your family is?" Clarissa's eyes were wide.

"I just don't want them to know how *evil* my family is," I said. "But anyway, maybe I can help you guys with your mortgage problems. I learned a lot about them. My mom deals with mortgages at her job too."

I actually had learned one set of information about mortgages from my parents, and another set of information from a teach-in I went to at Occupy Wall Street. Between the two, I figured I was practically an expert.

Clarissa tucked her hair behind her ears again. I was starting to think it was kind of cute. "If I bring you some paperwork, would you be able to look at it and see if it looks fraudulent?"

"I could try," I said. At last, I was going to have a chance to use my knowledge, for a good cause.

Out in the parking lot, I ran into Slobberin' Robert. He was slipping flyers under windshield wipers, probably flyers for some awful Christian band's show that a friend of his was in. "Wassup, dawg?" he said.

If he was willing to help some dumb guitarist pal, maybe he would help Desi.

"Hey, Slobbo, you know how Desi Kirchendorfer is running for homecoming queen?"

"That's girl stuff," Slobberin' Robert said. "Not my department."

"It is your department. Vote for her. Tell your friends to vote for her."

"I don't have any friends," he said. "I'm liked, but I'm not well-liked."

I hate when people who have a million friends say they have no friends. It's like when really skinny girls start talking about how fat they are.

"What about Desi? I guess she's not your friend either."

He smiled. "Okay, no homo, but even I have feelings. I really do like Desi Kirchendorfer. People always say people with Down syndrome are so sweet, and I have no idea what they're talking about. That girl is a regular spitfire. Do not cross her."

I couldn't believe I was almost-friends with someone who said *no homo*.

"Think about it like this," I said. "When you're forty years old and your teeth are falling out, do you want to remember how you helped a nice girl achieve her dream or how you were just a schmucky guy who did nothing?"

"I'm probably not going to live that long," Slobberin' Robert said, laughing.

"What makes you say that?"

"I drink, I do drugs, I drive afterward," he said. "It's a matter of time."

"That's terrible. You shouldn't do that." I was repulsed.

"Easy for you to say. How else am I supposed to get from point A to point B without driving?"

"No, I mean you shouldn't drink and drive," I said. It was hard for me to imagine how he could be so stupid. This view into his twisted mind was amazing. It was like I had seen something gross that I could never unsee.

He shook his head, still smiling.

"It might not just be you who dies," I pointed out. "You could take out a kid. A whole carful of kids."

He shivered but still kept smiling. "I surrender, I surrender. I'll help Desi."

Driving home, I had a long fantasy about me and Clarissa riding horses on a beach and then dismounting and kissing as the surf lapped at our feet. Ridiculous. What was I, twelve?

I was shocked when I got into my kitchen and met my mom there. She was never home at this hour. "Mom, is everything okay? Why are you here?"

"I'm packing for my business trip to Bermuda," my mom said. "Do you think I should wear my old-lady bathing suit with the skirt, or my tankini?"

"Old-lady one," I said. I was feeling much closer to her these days. I had submitted my application to Simon's Rock, and her essay had really helped our relationship. "Hey, Mom, did you ever ride a horse when you were a kid?"

"I took riding lessons at Claremont Stables," my mother said. "It was the only place that gave riding lessons in Manhattan. Why do you ask?"

"No reason," I said. "Maybe you can tell me a little bit about horses sometime."

"Sure," my mother said. She grabbed her purse, her garment bag, and her stylish little wheelie suitcase and headed for the door.

"Don't forget your passport," I said, but she was already gone.

CHAPTER THIRTEEN

Clarissa

On Tuesday, Lexie picked me up at the stable after work so we could discuss the foreclosure documents. I had scanned them and e-mailed them to her the night before. Her car was an eggplant purple Nissan Altima with a cloth interior, and it looked pretty old. I was surprised a girl with as much money as Lexie didn't drive a nicer car. But then again, it was probably all part of Lexie's angry girl act, like the way she dressed in clothes from Goodwill Super Store. How could she rail against capitalism and drive a Benzie?

"So, what you been up to?" she asked.

"Shoveling horse poop," I told her.

"What do they do with all that horse poop anyway?"

"A company from Newburgh picks it up and turns it into compost."

"I love compost," Lexie said.

"Okay, that's crazy," I said.

"Hey, my car is a safe space! No negativity," Lexie said.

I wasn't sure if we were insulting each other in a friendly way or for real. We fell silent.

Her house also surprised me. It was a big old Victorian

that had been restored. When I thought about it, that must have taken a lot of money, but it was so subtle looking. What was the point of being rich if you didn't show off and have an opulent house?

"My dad will probably be home later, but my mom's on a business trip," Lexie said.

I wasn't sure why that made me nervous. It wasn't like we were going to get busy or something. We were enemies. Okay, not anymore. Frenemies? Also, what the hell, *My dad will probably be home?* My dad always came home. I didn't have to speculate.

Lexie's room was bafflingly decorated with anime posters, old movie star pictures, and vintage flyers of concerts Lexie couldn't possibly have gone to unless she had seen Throwdown, whoever they were, when she was five. Over her bed was a big laminated poster of a hundred different kinds of butterflies, some of them circled in marker. Her bedspread was black with three skulls embroidered on it. Behind the skulls were angel wings and two pink guitars, crossed. Lexie followed my gaze and said defensively, "My mom got me that, okay? It's awful when she tries to guess my taste. It's always wrong."

"What's up with the butterfly poster?" I asked.

"Oh, I'm circling the ones I've seen," she said. "I love butterflies. They're so beautiful. It's like, why are people so into making up myths about God and Jesus and stuff that can't be seen? When there's so many miracles and beautiful things that are real and we can see them every day, like butterflies. Forget I said anything. I don't think we should discuss religion. You want some Yan Yan?"

"Some what?"

Lexie took out a little pink snack carton with Japanese writing on it. She peeled off the top and handed it to me. Inside were these breadstick-looking things and a separate compartment of pink stuff. The pink stuff was not unpleasantly fragrant and reminded me of those scented markers. I pulled out a stick. It had writing on it. It said: *Fox, Beware of Lies.* I dipped it in the strawberry goo and handed the package back to Lexie.

Lexie took one and read it off to me. "*Goat, be lucky.*" She blushed. Then she sat down on her bed and said in a businesslike way, "Okay, so here's the deal about your parents' mortgage. I think you could make a good case that it's a fraudulent mortgage."

I sat in the chair that was at Lexie's desk. "Really?"

"Yeah. First of all, that stuff about how your dad didn't know it was an adjustable-rate mortgage, and the teaser rate? That totally smacks of predatory lending. That's when they use deceptive practices and target uneducated people. No offense to your dad or anything."

"None taken," I said.

"Anyways. The fact that he was only three months late on his payments when they went into foreclosure is another red flag. Also, when your parents refinanced the house? They practically gave your parents more money than the house was even worth. They shouldn't have done that. They're not supposed to loan you more than you can pay back. That's just a bad practice. But all that stuff is more unethical than illegal. Here's the big thing. Your foreclosure documents were robo-signed."

"Excuse me?" Not understanding what people said to me about the mortgage was getting pretty old. I reached for another Yan Yan. This one said: *Starfish Star + Fish.*

"There was a whole thing on *60 Minutes* about this. Let me show you on YouTube—they can explain it better than I can," Lexie said.

What kind of sixteen-year-old watched *60 Minutes*?

That show was for old people. Lexie found the video she was looking for, and I was relieved to see it was really short.

But Lexie was right; the video explained everything very simply. Basically banks had given mortgages to anyone with a pulse, so now they had so many foreclosures they couldn't keep up with all the paperwork. So instead of having bank employees review the foreclosure documents and sign them the way they were supposed to, they hired a bunch of hairdressers and high-school students to sit around signing thousands of affidavits without even knowing what they were.

"I'm a little bit jealous of these robo-signers," I said, taking another Yan Yan. "They got nine bucks an hour just to sign papers."

I had a daydream of myself sitting in a nice cool bank, signing papers instead of cleaning stalls at Mrs. Astin's. Then I would come upon the documents for my own house, and I would just put them in the shredder.

"I think you're missing the point," Lexie said. "Robo-signing isn't legal, it's fraudulent. It invalidates the whole foreclosure."

"Wait, wait," I said. "You mean we could keep our house if our documents were robo-signed?"

Lexie grinned. "I *know* your documents were robo-signed. That's the beauty of it. There are lists on the Internet of all the known robo-signers. One page is called *You Know It's Robo-Signed If Their Name Is*. And it was right there on the list. Charmaine Marchesi." She flipped through the documents I had scanned and shook the page at me, stabbing at the signature line.

"Charmaine Marchesi," I read. "Huh, what do you know?"

"There's something else too," Lexie said. "I believe the bank is missing papers they need in order to foreclose on you. Where's the promissory note? A lot of times when the loan changes hands over and over like yours did, the lenders are so badly organized that they lose this important paper. This is something that could make a judge throw out the foreclosure."

"Wow. So how do I get it to court? I'm not sure how much time we have."

"I don't know that part," Lexie admitted. "I would start by sending a letter to the bank saying you're on to them and you intend to take it to court. And then go on our local TV station and explain your plight."

"I'm not sure about that," I said. Her ideas seemed a bit half-baked. Like something from a kids' movie where people win just because they're right.

"And also look for a good lawyer. But obviously your parents really need to be the ones who do that."

"I'm sure they will, when I tell them everything you told me," I said. "Thank you, Lexie. This is a big deal."

I felt a lightening around my heart. Maybe my family wouldn't be cast into the street. My gratitude was genuine and vast. I got up and threw my arms around Lexie.

A sensation like an electric current went through my body. I experienced a strong urge that didn't come from my brain— but from somewhere else—to push Lexie down on the bed and kiss her. Oh, my. I tore myself away from Lexie, and I had to make myself do it.

"All right, I gotta go," I said.

"Wait, stay," Lexie said. "Have another Yan Yan." She took one herself. "*Mouse, do not be timid*," she read.

"No, I have to go to the library," I said at random.

"I'll drive you," Lexie said. "Unless someone is coming to pick you up?"

I shook my head. No one was coming to take me to the

library because I had just conceived of the idea one second ago. But I would be safer in Lexie's car than in her bedroom. Lexie would be busy driving, so I couldn't kiss her or paw at her.

"Are you going to the Dover Plains library?" she asked.

"Yes. Yes, I am. That is exactly the library where I've been planning to go."

I calmed down a little in the car. We were listening to these two soothing female vocalists. I wondered what would be so wrong if I *did* kiss Lexie. She was much nicer than I had originally thought. And she was kind of cute. I peeked over at her strong profile, her spiky blue hair. Her pale arms gripping the steering wheel. Her well-shaped legs.

"What?" Lexie said, glancing at me. "Why are you staring at me?"

"Me, staring?" I said.

"Yeah, you were staring at my legs."

"Uh, let's see." I was not good at lying. "Oh, I was just thinking you'd make a good horseback rider," I stuttered out.

"You really think so?" Lexie sounded pleased. And like she'd bought my story.

"You ever done it? Horseback riding, I mean?" I asked.

"No, I never did. I was kind of thinking recently I'd like to try it. Maybe you could teach me."

This whole conversation sounded like double entendre. Either Lexie was flirting with me, making fun of me, or she was genuinely interested in horses. I wondered what she really thought of me. Did she think I was dumb because I didn't know anything about mortgages and butterflies or whatever?

"Who is this singing?" I asked, to change the subject.

"The Indigo Girls," Lexie said. "If you're going to be a real lesbian, you have to learn about the Indigo Girls."

"I'm bisexual, I told you," I said.

"I don't trust bisexuals," Lexie said. "If I was dating a bisexual, what would stop her from deciding to date a boy instead?"

"I can't believe you," I said. "What's to stop anyone from deciding to date someone else instead? Bisexual doesn't mean sleeps around. It doesn't mean you have to date a boy and a girl at the same time." Why was Lexie talking about dating a bisexual? What did that mean? "It's totally unfair that bi people face discrimination not just from straight people but from gay people too sometimes."

"What you say makes sense," Lexie said reluctantly. That was something I liked about her. She'd say these dumb things, but she was willing to admit when she was wrong. "I guess I just don't believe bisexuals really exist," Lexie said. "Like, girls who say they're bi are really gay and won't admit it, or straight and just goofing around."

"Well, we do exist," I said. "Wouldn't I know whether or not I exist? They say it's a spectrum. Sexuality is a spectrum. Like autism."

"Like autism?" Lexie repeated doubtfully.

"There's a range of where you can be. So picture a football field. Way over on one end are the people who only like people of the opposite sex. And way over on the other end are people who only like people of the same sex. And then a lot of people are strung out somewhere in the middle."

"I can picture that," said Lexie. "But this football field only has two ends, two genders. The gender binary isn't real. Did you learn about that on the Internet yet?"

"Maybe it's actually a series of wraparound, intersecting football fields," I suggested. "To accommodate many genders and many combinations."

"That's a remarkable image," Lexie said.

It was good she was saying that, right? But then again,

maybe it meant she thought I was an idiot and she hadn't expected me to come up with something remarkable. If smart people are so smart, then why don't they realize they're not the only ones who are smart?

We were driving on Route 22, past the old abandoned Harlem Valley Psychiatric Center. It was a long row of red-brick buildings with mesh over the windows and a neglected and decaying air.

"That place gives me the creeps," Lexie said.

"Me too," I said. "Think of all the bad things that went on in there. If any place is haunted, it's got to be that one."

"Yeah, they would lock you up for anything back in the day," Lexie said. "People got institutionalized for being gay."

"People with Down syndrome got institutionalized at birth," I said. "They were locked up on some back ward and treated like garbage and they usually didn't live too long." I shivered, and Lexie turned the heat up in her car.

On that cheerful note, we pulled into the parking lot of the Dover Plains Library. It was a bright, contemporary building as different from the abandoned state hospital as a building could be.

"Thanks for driving me," I said. I didn't know why I had said I had to go to the library. Now my mom or dad would have to drive all the way here to pick me up, and they would be cross. I would have to imply I was doing a school project or something, and I hated lying.

Lexie leaned across the car and hugged me. "Good luck with the mortgage stuff. Let me know what I can do."

Surely Lexie could feel the electricity in the car between us. "See you at school," I said.

My heart was pounding like a jackhammer as I walked into the library. Riding in a friend's car should not cause these heart-attack symptoms.

I slumped into a chair to think. The reason I was so panicked about being attracted to Lexie was I didn't understand why I liked her. In fact, I didn't understand her at all. With Slobberin' Robert, I started going out with him just because I thought he was really cute, the way his hair fell down across his dark brown eyes and all that. Then we ended up being a terrible match. I never did figure out why he was so moody and uncommunicative. That was a road I never wanted to go down again. Just liking someone was not enough. There were certain things about Lexie I couldn't get over, like her misspelled tattoo and her harsh attitude. I needed to learn more about Lexie, to see if we were compatible. I wished there was a book about Lexie in the library. What was she all about? I had heard Lexie say she was a radical. That was a polite word for Communist, I was pretty sure.

I walked over to the help desk. "Hi! I want to read a book by a Communist," I told the bearded librarian.

"Any Communist in particular?" he asked.

"Whoever is the most famous Communist," I told him.

"The most famous Communist? I guess that would probably be Lenin," said the librarian.

"I'll take something by him," I said. I had totally heard of him, so he was definitely famous.

He pecked at his keyboard. "The only work by Lenin we have in this branch is *What Is To Be Done?*"

"Awesome," I said. I liked that name. It would tell me what to do.

The librarian led me through the stacks and pulled out a book covered in brown library binding. "Here it is!"

I looked at the book doubtfully. It looked dense and boring. It even seemed to give off a musty smell.

"I assume this is for a school project," he said.

"Oh no," I assured him. "My school wouldn't do any

kind of crazy project like that. It's because there's a girl I'm interested in, and she's a Communist. I think."

"Ah, okay," said the librarian. "In that case, let me recommend another book for you."

He didn't even have to look this one up, he just led me straight over to a different area of the stacks and handed me another book. It was called *Teens: Being Gay, Lesbian, Bisexual, or Transgender—Friendship, Dating, and Relationships*.

"You can read it here if you don't want to bring it home," he said.

"Thanks," I said. I could see he was all excited about making a positive impact on a real Teen Who Was Gay, Lesbian, Bisexual, or Transgender. I should tell more people that I liked girls if it was going to make them so smiley.

"Anything else you need?" he asked hopefully. I saw now he was actually a young guy. His Abraham Lincoln beard had thrown me off. He must be some kind of hipster.

"I guess. My parents are going to pick me up here, and I need a book to make it look like I was getting something for school. Not something queer or by a Communist."

Without a word he led me to the school assignments shelf and selected a copy of *The Scarlet Letter*.

"Thanks so much," I said, taking my stack of books over to the counter to check them out. The library was great. They really waited on you hand and foot.

I texted my dad and asked him if he could pick me up. While I was waiting, I surfed the Internet on a library computer. I found a list of Marxist/Leninist terminology that would surely help me understand what went on in Lexie's mind. Some of the phrases sounded really entertaining, like *lumpenproletariat, enemy of the people, foco revolutionary theory*, and *capitalist roader*.

My dad finally showed up, looking grim and tired, with

lines etched into his face I'd never seen before. I had left *The Scarlet Letter* on top, but he looked at all the books I had and blanched.

"Pum'kin, just because we're having these troubles with the house, I don't want your life to get all screwed up," he said hoarsely.

"Nobody's life is screwed up," I told him.

We drove home in silence.

CHAPTER FOURTEEN

Lexie

After I spent forty minutes on Clarissa's Facebook page, looking at every single photo, I decided it was officially time to give up my campaign to forget Clarissa. I deleted my *Either You Don't Love Me or I Don't Love You* Spotify playlist and created a new *I Don't Want To Get Over You* playlist. Ovid had let me down, but I didn't care. I really liked Clarissa. She made me want to take care of her and protect her from all harm. The crap her family was going through with their house was so messed up. I wanted to get my personal revenge on the heartless banks and processors who were ripping off the Kirchendorfers. I had known banks created the subprime mortgage crisis and then received billions in bailouts while homeowners had to default. But it was one thing to read about it in *The Occupied Wall Street Journal*, and another to know someone it was happening to.

The more I thought about it, the angrier I got. It was nine thirty and my dad wasn't home from work yet. I realized there was truly nothing to stop me from acting on my desire for revenge. I remembered a poem that had been in my English book last year called "Factory Windows Are Always Broken" that went like this:

Factory windows are always broken.
Other windows are let alone.
No one throws through the chapel-window
The bitter, snarling, derisive stone.

The idea bloomed in my mind like a flower. I had thought about it a lot, but never had the nerve. I dressed in black jeans and a baggy black Rise Against hoodie, inside out so the writing and patches were hidden. I tied a kerchief around my neck cowgirl style. I looked for gloves too, but I couldn't find any, so I put on winter mittens. I went into the garden where I had a pile of rocks I had been collecting to create a butterfly garden. The idea was to have an arrangement of nectar-providing plants continuously in bloom, with flat rocks for the butterflies to rest on so they could bask in the sun. So far I hadn't gotten any further with this project than collecting stones and planting some milkweed. I picked a nice big rock, but not so big I couldn't throw it.

I wanted to write a note, but I wasn't sure that was a good idea. People don't throw rocks through your window because they love you, so I thought my message would be reasonably clear. Then I took off my mittens so I could Google the closest MegaBank. Last thing I did was mix some dirt from the garden in a pot with water and splash the mud over my car's plates to obscure the numbers.

It was a seven-minute drive. I parked in the mini-mall next to the plaza where the MegaBank was. It felt weird to wear mittens in late September when the air was still warm. I walked over the planter that divided the two parking lots from each other, carrying my rock. There wasn't a single car in the lot, but I pulled the bandanna up over my mouth and nose in case there were security cameras. It was hard to do with mittens on and I started to feel panicked, like I couldn't breathe properly through the bandanna.

When I heaved the rock, MegaBank's plate glass window exploded. There was something fundamentally satisfying about it, but the sound of breaking glass was so loud, I got scared. I ran like a rabbit back to my car. I could see that the remaining glass in the window was cracked into a jagged spiderweb. I couldn't believe I had actually done it, as if I had thought something would happen between the part where I threw the rock and the part where it hit the window. I had a kind of feeling of unreality, like I had entered a new life.

It was hard not to speed on my way home. I alternated between triumph and paranoia. Surely the police would knock on my door any minute? I knew what I had done was probably not going to make a difference to MegaBank, but it was better to do something, anything, than to sit around doing sweet nothing.

My dad still wasn't home. I washed my license plate, changed into my jammies, and put away all my crime clothes. My dad came home when I was making myself a bedtime cocoa, and I made one for him too, except he put Baileys in his. I took mine to my bedroom, but it took me a couple hours to calm down enough to fall asleep.

My cell phone woke me up a few hours later. My ringtone was Dillinger Four's "New Punk Fashions For The Spring Formal." Which is kind of hard to sleep through. I was having a weird dream about an alien being who had taken over my neighborhood and was forcing people to meld with it. Then a taxi went by and I got into it, and I thought I was going to escape. The ringtone stopped. Gone to voice mail. I slipped back into the dream. Now the taxi driver was asking me to interface with the alien mind. This dream was awful. I was grateful when Dillinger Four started up again, and I groped for the phone.

Even with the glowing screen it was hard to find the talk button. "Hello?" I said in a husky voice full of sleep.

"It's Clarissa," the voice said.

"Clarissa?" I said. I didn't think we had that kind of relationship, where she would call in the middle of the night. I stupidly wondered if it was about me throwing a rock through the bank window.

"Yeah, you know, the bisexual girl whose house is being foreclosed on?"

"I know who you are," I said. I was starting to wake up. "What time is it?"

"It's three thirty a.m.," Clarissa said. "The point is, something bad happened. I had to tell you."

"Bad?" Now I was totally awake. "What happened? Are you okay?"

"I'm fine," Clarissa said. "It didn't happen to me. It happened to Slobberin' Robert."

I had an uneasy feeling about this. As a general rule I didn't really care what happened to Slobberin' Robert. So this must be something quite bad.

"He's not dead," Clarissa reassured me. "But he was in a terrible car accident. You know Dead Man's Curve on Route 22 as you're entering Millerton from the south?"

"Yeah," I said. It was a sharp curve right next to a solid wall of rock. The wall was painted in yellow-and-black checkers. You were supposed to slow down to fifteen miles an hour, but no one ever did. Fifteen miles an hour is really slow.

"He crashed straight into it, going full speed. What the hell was he was doing out there at that hour? There's not much going on in Millerton at two a.m. on a Wednesday night. It was just him in the car. They took him to Sharon Hospital in Connecticut because it was the closest. Anyway, what I heard is he's in a coma."

"Oh no, that's awful," I said. "Poor Slob—I mean, poor Robert." It seemed wrong to call him Slobberin' Robert when he was in a coma. "Is he going to be okay?"

"I don't know," Clarissa said. "One of his legs is totally shattered, like it's just in bits on the inside. They had to pry him out of the wreck with the Jaws of Life. It was Jenna who told me. Her dad is a doctor there, so he called her. Then she called me because she knew I'd want to know. Because I used to go out with him and everything."

My unspoken question hung in the air. *And why exactly are you calling me?*

"And I'm calling you, oh, I guess for two reasons. I just needed to tell someone. Talk to someone. I think Jenna called me to be nice. But I'm not sure, to be honest. I wanted to talk to someone who…who…who cares about…Anyway."

"I do care about you," I said. Was this conversation real or part of my alien dream?

"And the second reason is I think you kind of connected with Slobberin' Robert."

"I don't know about that," I said. "We only ever talked about—"

"Movies and sometimes TV, I know. You told me."

"He has lots of friends, the soccer team, the God squad, all those loadies who get high in the parking lot. I'm not even really his friend," I said. I didn't want to be his friend because then this would somehow be my fault. I was already starting to feel guilty about the conversation we'd had where he casually told me he liked to drink and drive.

"But I think you really get him," Clarissa said. "He seemed

very himself with you, very comfortable. Slobberin' Robert, he's a funny guy, he is. It's hard for him to relate to people, I think. Usually he's putting on some kind of act. He thinks everyone has an agenda. You don't have an agenda. Unless it's a Marxist agenda."

"I don't have a Marxist agenda," I said. "This is weird. I feel like we're talking about him like he's dead."

"He never wore a seat belt," Clarissa said. "Same as *your* ex, Ramone. Listen, I'm sorry I woke you up."

"It's totally fine," I said. I wanted to tell her I'd be happy to hear from her day and night, about anything, but obviously I couldn't say that.

"But is this supposed to be like a telephone chain or something?" I asked. "Everyone is going to find out tomorrow."

"No, no," Clarissa said. "I just wanted to tell you. I'll see you at school."

"Okay. I'm really sorry. I hope he'll be all right. Try to get some sleep, Clarissa."

I lay awake, thinking about Slobberin' Robert. Whoever his real friends were, the kids who cared about him the most, they were probably sleeping peacefully, not knowing that someone they loved was in a coma. Maybe he had aunts and uncles who had known him his whole life, and they didn't even know yet. But somehow I knew. I was glad those people got to get more sleep, have some more hours before their lives were changed. I felt some kind of weird responsibility, though, as if I was holding a vigil by being awake and knowing about it. It was quite upsetting, but I didn't think I really had the right to be upset. It was odd, too, that I had gone out to vandalize MegaBank the same night as Slobberin' Robert got into a smashup.

I was sure he had been drunk, or high, or both. Slobberin' Robert must be an unhappy, seriously screwed-up person. Yet it seemed like Clarissa was saying the athlete and the Christian and the druggie were all an act. And the real him liked to talk about screen trivia. It didn't seem like much of a core for a person to have.

How could you ever really understand another person? Two weeks ago I had hated Clarissa Kirchendorfer. Now she seemed like the brightest star in the galaxy. How was it possible to be so wrong about someone? Maybe if there were some kind of translating device, where you could learn people's inner thoughts, it would be possible to feel sympathy and understanding for anyone.

Vandalizing the MegaBank branch seemed like a dream. I couldn't believe it had just been a few hours ago.

❖

School that day was awful. And not because I hadn't gotten much sleep. The first thing was an assembly where the principal announced Slobberin' Robert's accident to the whole school.

"This is a terrible tragedy," the principal said dolefully. "Yet we can be hopeful Robert will recover. This should be an object lesson, a moral parable even, to you, not to drive under the influence."

He couldn't seem to get his tone quite right. Part of me wanted to be mad Slobberin' Robert's good name was being besmirched—nobody mentioned any proof he had been drunk or high. But in my heart I was pretty certain he had been.

A few girls around me started crying. At first I was kind of touched. But then it started to seem like there was something insincere about the flood of tears. Like people were crying for effect. People seemed to be competing about who was the most upset about Slobberin' Robert. Suddenly everyone was his best friend, and he was the most popular boy in school.

Some of the teachers gave over part of their classes to letting students share their emotions about Slobberin' Robert's accident. I didn't want to share my emotions; I just wanted to feel them quietly by myself. But my classmates had a lot to say. They seemed to be describing a boy I had never met, a selfless, caring individual whose perfect life had been spoiled by tragedy. A few people were even talking about how Slobberin' Robert had supported Desi Kirchendorfer's homecoming campaign. *Did you hear how he wanted to be homecoming king with one of the special-ed girls? That is just so amazing.*

I really wanted to talk to Clarissa. I didn't know how to assess my own feelings. Maybe I was just being too cynical. I knew I could trust Clarissa because I knew now Clarissa spoke from the heart if anyone ever did. But what if Clarissa started spouting nonsense about Slobberin' Robert being a martyr like some of the other girls had?

When I got to the cafeteria at my lunch period, Clarissa was standing by the line, anxiously scanning the crowd. Her blossoming smile when she saw me made me feel like a million bucks. I was the one Clarissa had been looking for.

Clarissa embraced me. It seemed like every time we said hello or good-bye now, we hugged. But unlike last time, today I didn't feel sexual energy so thick I could almost bite into it. Now it was just a soft warmth. Clarissa's hair had a distinctive lavender shampoo smell I was growing to love. I thought if someone waved that smell under my nose it would make me happy before I knew why.

"Will you come eat with me in the crevice?" Clarissa said. "I can't take how crazy it is here. I got us some Hostess Fruit Pies for lunch."

"Okay," I said. I hadn't eaten a Hostess Fruit Pie since elementary school. Could they really be vegan?

The crevice was the small anteroom outside the art room. I didn't go there much because it was really a place for people to meet in groups. Mostly art chicks hung out there, but they didn't seem to be very possessive about the place.

There were a couple of girls gossiping intensely, sitting on a bookshelf right next to the door of the art room, but the little round table with chairs was miraculously unoccupied. Clarissa forked over my Fruit Pie. It was lemon.

"Everyone is losing their minds," Clarissa said.

"That's what I'm thinking too."

"I think Slobberin' Robert would be almost offended if he knew what people are saying about him. Also, people are referring to him as Robbie. I've never heard him called Robbie in my life. People keep coming up to me and pawing me and saying how sorry they are. I *am* really upset, but I'm not, like, his widow. And their weird behavior is not helping. This girl Haileigh Askegaard who I know from equestrian was, like, sobbing in my arms, and talking about him like they were really close. And I know for a fact Slobberin' Robert didn't like her. I heard him say more than once that she was a brainless zombie and he was just waiting for her limbs to start rotting off. Which, by the way, is exactly the kind of thing he says. He's not the saintly Robbie Gelisano that people are discussing."

"I'm so glad to hear you say these things," I said. "I don't know why all these people are faking it."

"Yeah," Clarissa said. "It's odd. It almost seems like some kind of crazy mass delusion."

"That can really happen. I read about this girl in England almost a hundred years ago who believed she could levitate herself," I said. "And all these other people believed it too. It was like group hypnosis. And then one day the crowd trampled her to death."

"That's awful," Clarissa said. "I wonder if she really could levitate herself."

"I don't believe in that kind of thing," I said. "I'm a rationalist. I believe in empiricism, in the scientific philosophy sense."

"Rationalist, empiricism," Clarissa repeated. As if she were memorizing essay topics or book titles.

"What about you?" I asked. "I mean, do you believe someone could levitate?" Hanging around Clarissa made me vaguely aware of how often I spouted my opinions in a dogmatic way. And didn't even ask Clarissa what *she* thought. Also it was like some part of my brain was interested in talking about levitation and empiricism, but the rest of my brain was just screaming, *Take me in your arms!*

"I try to keep an open mind," Clarissa said. "It would be an amazing world if there really were miracles. The pastor at my church thinks they're real. But I don't know, sometimes he's a little bonkers."

"Let me ask you this," I said. "If this girl really could levitate herself, then how did she get trampled by a hysterical crowd?"

"Good point," said Clarissa. "How did you hear about this levitating girl?"

"I just read it in a novel. You know, not for school."

"Wow," Clarissa said. "I hardly ever read. Although I just got some library books—" She stopped abruptly. "Why are you doing so bad in school if you're so smart?"

"I just hate school," I said. "Doesn't everyone? It's so awful. I'm not willing to waste my time studying and doing the homework."

Once again, I sounded like a snot nose. I wondered if Clarissa even really liked me. She knew I liked her—on the phone last night she had said, or almost said, that I cared about her. But did she care about me?

"I guess most people don't like school. But everyone else just does it anyway. Maybe you have some obscure learning disability," Clarissa said.

I shrugged.

"Listen, speaking of hating school, I can't handle it here today," Clarissa said. "It's too creepy. I'm going to skip. Take a mental-health day. You want to come with?"

"Sure," I said, pleased. It's always good to skip school, but especially with a pretty girl. Spending the rest of the day alone with Clarissa was an unexpected present after this tough morning.

CHAPTER FIFTEEN

Clarissa

We ended up going to Lexie's house, with my bike in the back of her car. Even though Lexie had a wrench set, which she claimed was a must-have for lesbians, it took a long time to figure out how to get the wheel off to fit it in the trunk. When we went inside, a woman was cooking in the kitchen. The food looked way too healthy to taste good. I smiled and said hello to her, but she ignored me. She did say hello to Lexie. I realized she was some kind of domestic servant, not a member of Lexie's family. I thought all my horseback-riding friends came from fancy families, but none of them had servants who cooked for them. It made me uncomfortable.

"That's Mrs. Álvaz," Lexie explained as we headed up the stairs. "She's the housekeeper. I wonder what she thinks we're doing here."

Suddenly I wondered what we were doing here.

In Lexie's room we settled ourselves into the same configuration as before: she sat on the bed and I sat in the chair.

"Do you wonder if Slobberin' Robert was trying to kill himself?" Lexie asked hesitantly.

"It's so awful, but I do kind of think so," I said. "I mean, driving too fast at night, maybe he crashed into Dead Man's Curve on purpose. It's not like he doesn't know it's there. He's been around it a hundred times. We used to go to the McDonald's in Millerton a lot, or the Mexican taco place. Or maybe just unconsciously he wanted to hurt himself. If you're doing all that self-destructive stuff, what's really going on in your head? I did find out when the visiting hours are at the hospital."

"I don't know if I want to visit someone in a coma," Lexie said. "I think I'd be too creeped out. And how would it help?"

"He might be aware of your presence," I said.

I was hyperaware of Lexie's presence right then. Her body was calling to my body, like those little magnetic Scottie dogs. If I didn't get out of her bedroom, I was going to climb right on top of her, and I still hadn't resolved any of my doubts about her.

"Maybe we need to go outside," I said. "You know, the calming effects of nature and everything."

"That's a great idea. I can show you my new compost pile."

"Um, okay."

We didn't have to pass Mrs. Álvaz to go out into the backyard, which was good because I'd started to feel guilty about skipping school. It was pretty nice out, and I felt just right in my jeans and cashmere sweater. Lexie showed me the compost pile, which didn't even have any bugs or smell bad. It was just dirt with some food scraps in it. The garden was beautifully manicured. Even though most of the flowers were dead because it was fall, I could tell this was some kind of showplace.

An orange-and-black butterfly flew by, coming to rest on a rock with its wings outstretched. "You must have seen that one before," I said to Lexie. "That kind is really common. What are they called again?"

"Oh, that's a monarch." Then she frowned. "But a lot of them have left for Mexico in big packs by now."

"What, they go on vacation?"

"Kind of. They fly thousands of miles. Trees in Mexico get literally covered in butterflies as they gather together. They go back to the exact same trees in the Sierra Madres every year, even though it's actually different butterflies because their lives are short. They just know somehow."

"That's crazy," I said.

Lexie was still scowling at the butterfly, going closer to get a better look. "There's something wrong with this one's wing. Maybe it can't keep up with the others and that's why it's still here. I've got to fix it."

"Fix it? What are you, a butterfly surgeon?"

She didn't even smile. "Yeah." She darted toward a cunning little shed. Soon she was back, holding a butterfly net. Swish, the net came down on the butterfly. She grabbed the bottom of the net as the butterfly pattered its wings against the top. Now that the butterfly was trapped in the net, she headed for the house.

Mrs. Álvaz was cleaning the entryway. "Oh no, Alexandra!" she said. "Your mother said no more bugs in the house."

"No, it's okay," Lexie said vaguely. We went to the kitchen, where she got a glass and trapped the butterfly inside. I couldn't believe it when she popped the glass in the fridge. "This will slow the butterfly down and make it sluggish so it's easier to work on," she explained.

"I didn't know your name is Alexandra," I said.

"She's the only one who calls me that," Lexie said.

After a few minutes Lexie took the butterfly out of the

fridge, and we headed back up the stairs to her room. She pulled down the blinds, further setting the scene for seduction.

"That will make the butterfly think it's evening, and it will be more relaxed."

I told myself to get my head out of the gutter and focus on this poor injured, refrigerated bug.

"Now we have to operate," Lexie said. "Will you be my assistant?"

"Sure."

She picked up the butterfly by the wings. "Part of one wing is missing," she said. "It must have gotten torn off somehow. The wings have to be symmetrical to work right. If less of it was missing, I would just cut the other wing to make them match, but there's too much gone. I'm going to have to glue on a new wing."

This sounded crazy.

Lexie pulled a tote bag from under her desk. Out of it she brought a towel and a wire hanger with the hook part twisted into a loop. She cleared a space on the desk, laid out the towel, put the butterfly on the towel, and plopped the small wire loop over the butterfly so its body was pinned with wings at either side. Now I could see that one wing ended too soon in a jagged edge because a big hunk was gone. She gently tugged on the wings until they were both splayed out. Then she weighted down the hanger with a stapler that was lying on her desk.

"Okay, everything I need is in there," she said, gesturing to the tote bag. "Can you give me the butterfly wings?"

Feeling like I was losing all connection with reality, I looked in the tote and found a Ziploc bag filled with wings. Gross. "Where did you get these?" I asked, handing it to her.

"Butterflies only live about a month, so I collect these from the dead ones." She picked a wing out of the bag. It was black and yellow, not orange, and it didn't match the butterfly she had pinned under the coat hanger at all. "I'm all out of monarch wings," she said. "This one's a tawny crescent wing. It's okay if they're not the same kind of wing as long as they're basically symmetrical."

"It kind of clashes," I observed.

"Scissors," she said, holding out her hand. I snapped the pair of scissors handle first into her hand, feeling like an OR nurse.

"The edge of the wing needs to be straight to repair it," she said, snipping off the end of the damaged wing. "Don't worry, it doesn't hurt them."

"How do you know?"

She laid the new wing over the old and cut it so it just barely overlapped. I was struck by how deft and sure her hands were with the delicate wing. "Glue," she barked. "And a toothpick." I handed them to her. The glue was a contact adhesive like my dad used to repair the ceiling upholstery of cars. Very carefully Lexie applied the glue with the toothpick onto the back of the new wing.

"Tweezers!" She held the wing in the tweezers and laid the new wing precisely where it needed to go. The body of the butterfly flapped, but it was trapped by the coat hanger. It was kind of disgusting. Lexie pressed down on the wing.

"Cornstarch, please. I need to soak up the extra glue." She sprinkled this on the wing. The wing looked pretty strange now that it was two different colors and dusted with powder. She lifted off the coat hanger and picked up the butterfly by both wings. Its tiny legs cycled furiously. She gently pressed the wings, making sure the repair was complete. Then she let it go. It floated onto her hand and sat there, flapping its wings slowly.

"It's totally stunned," I said. "It has no idea what just happened."

"I feel like Dr. Frankenstein," she said, cracking a smile now that surgery was over. She pulled the shades back up and opened the window. "Go, little patchwork monarch, go. Maybe now our little friend will make it to Mexico."

"You must really love butterflies," I said.

"I really do." Her pale face lit up. "They're so beautiful. All they do is bring happiness and pollinate plants." The butterfly flew off out the window, and Lexie closed it and went to sit on her bed.

The last defenses in my heart finally softened to Lexie. Her true nature was now displayed to me. She couldn't be bad or mean if she loved defenseless little creatures so much that she would spend her time healing an animal that only lived for a few weeks. I liked animals that could show affection, like horses and dogs. It would never occur to me to help an insect. Lexie had a gruff exterior, but she had a heart of gold.

Now I really wanted to kiss her.

So I said, "I really want to kiss you."

"Awesome," she said and patted the bed. "Come here."

"But wait!" I said. I was nervous. "I have a few questions for you."

Now she looked nervous too. "I don't have any diseases or anything."

"Why do you have a misspelled tattoo on your hand?" I blurted out.

"What?" She looked at the sXe on her hand. "It's not misspelled! That means straight edge. Straight edge is a kind of punk rock where you don't smoke, drink, or do drugs."

"It's a kind of music?"

"It's a whole lifestyle that goes along with the music," Lexie said.

"I never knew punks could be such clean citizens," I said.

She patted the bed again. "Come sit next to me and I'll tell you all about it."

"What if you change your mind someday? What will you do about your tattoo?"

"Oh, that will never happen," she said, and her naïveté made me feel even more gooey toward her.

So no misspelled tattoo, that was good. I went and sat beside her on the bed. She put one hand on my shoulder. Her touch seemed to go right through my skin to the deepest parts of me.

"I have another question," I said. "Are you a Communist?"

She laughed. "No, and that's your last question." She leaned forward and time seemed to slow down. Our faces drifted closer and closer. I saw that Lexie's eyes were closed. I smelled her breath—minty fresh—and then her lips brushed mine. We kissed, and I wrapped my arms around her. Lexie was so warm, she was throwing off heat like a stove. I felt so good it was like I was coming unglued. Our kisses became slow and lingering, and I could feel the heat through my whole body. I stroked Lexie's cheek and couldn't get over how soft her skin was. I couldn't help comparing her smooth cheek to Slobberin' Robert's stubbly one.

My phone rang. I theoretically heard it but it seemed like it was coming from another dimension because I was completely enmeshed in the wonder of being in Lexie's arms. Her lips against mine were more than everything. She was running her hand down my back. Her hand slipped into the back pocket of my jeans.

The phone rang a bunch more times. Finally we stopped kissing long enough for me to fumblingly turn it off without even looking at it. Then we got back to it.

Chapter Sixteen

Lexie

At some point we took a break from kissing and just lay on the bed, staring at each other. Clarissa looked super cute with her hair all messy and falling out of her ponytail. There was something about Clarissa that made me feel protective and tender. When I was with Ramone, we had been like tigers, two feisty lady tigers. Nothing tender.

Clarissa was gazing at me with an intense expression, her hair framing her face. With my eyes, I traced each little tendril of hair. We held each other's gaze, and it was almost like we were talking to each other without saying a word. I was communicating to her that she was the most beautiful girl I had ever seen, and weirdly she seemed to be beaming that right back at me.

I was super self-conscious of the fact that Clarissa had kissed Ramone, that Ramone was the only other girl either of us had ever kissed. Ramone was like some horrible vector. I touched Clarissa's incredibly soft hair, trying to focus on the girl who was actually in front of me and not my ex. It was crazy to me that all of a sudden I could actually kiss Clarissa and stroke her hair.

"I really like you," Clarissa said.

"I really like you too," I said. We smiled at each other like we were saying brilliant things.

"Let's go out on a date," Clarissa said.

I laughed. "Now?"

"No, I'm asking you out on a future date."

"Okay," I said. Ramone had never taken me out on an official date. I told myself to stop thinking about Ramone. I supposed it was only natural, but it had to stop. I wondered if Clarissa was comparing me to Slobberin' Robert.

"I can't go out Friday night because I'm volunteering at this disco thing Desi goes to. You could come, but I don't think that would be a great date. Let's go to brunch on Saturday morning. You want to go to Cracker Barrel? The one in Fishkill? Their breakfast is amazing."

"Cracker Barrel? Are you joking?" I asked.

"No. Why? What's wrong with Cracker Barrel?"

"They're totally famous for discriminating against gays and lesbians. They used to officially fire people for being gay. Like, it said on the pink slip, *Reason fired: she is gay.*"

"No way! I never heard that."

"They don't do it anymore, not in the last few years. But they're still one of the worst places for gay people to work. There's a group that rates all the big companies, and Cracker Barrel comes in almost dead last."

"I had no idea." She snuggled closer to me. "I feel bad. I have breakfast with my parents there all the time."

I kissed her on her nose. "You weren't to know." Clarissa seemed like such an alien creature to me. Why would anyone want to have breakfast at some hokey franchise anyway?

"How about the Red Line Diner?" Clarissa suggested. "That's right next to Cracker Barrel. We go there sometimes when Cracker Barrel is too crowded."

"It's called the Red Line Diner? What the hell?"

"And now what's wrong with that?" Clarissa asked.

"Redlining is when banks deny mortgages to black people based on race. Why would they call a restaurant that?"

"I don't want to think about mortgages anymore," Clarissa said and kissed me again. "Turn off that part of your brain, please. This morning my dad told me he got a letter that said we had been accepted into a new payment program. So I think we're okay. Which is good because my dad didn't want to do any of the things you said, like go see a lawyer. Can you think of a restaurant you don't object to where we can go on a date?"

I wanted to pick a place Clarissa would like, similar to the places she had mentioned. I didn't want to seem like some kind of left-wing ogre who hated everything. "Friendly's?" I suggested, and she nodded.

Being with Clarissa was like dating a Martian, because she was so different from me. But a beautiful Martian, who made me feel sparkly on the inside. It was amazing that I could actually communicate with Clarissa, connect with her even though we were so unlike each other. I had never felt this connected to Ramone, not even when we had been going out for months. First love had seemed like the best thing in the world, but maybe really second love was better.

I wanted to kiss Clarissa more and really go at it, but I was worried about how she thought of me. I didn't want to seem like a sex maniac. When I had been with Ramone, she had been the experienced one who took the lead, and I had been the enthusiastic go-along girl. Was I going to have to be the one who took the lead here?

This feeling, though. Maybe I was in love with Clarissa. I certainly wasn't going to say anything about it. It would be foolhardy to say *Maybe I'm in love with you*. But I wanted to do something to commemorate this.

I twisted off my evil-eye ring. It had a fat, glittering yellow stone in the center of the eye.

"Here," I said, handing it to Clarissa. "I want you to have this."

Clarissa laughed. "What? Are you proposing?" A flush was rising to her cheeks.

"No, of course not," I said. "This is an I-really-like-you ring. A we've-been-together-for-half-an-hour ring."

"Thank you," Clarissa said, taking it. She slid it on her ring finger but it was a bit loose. I hadn't realized until now what long, slender fingers Clarissa had. The ring looked warm against Clarissa's tanned skin. I have a corpse-like pallor, which is hard to accessorize.

"Maybe I should put it on a chain and wear it as a necklace," Clarissa said.

I knew necklaces were the kiss of death. "Just wear it, if you want," I told her.

Then I heard the front door slam.

"Hello, Mrs. Ganz," I heard Mrs. Álvaz saying loudly. My mom actually kept her maiden name but Mrs. Álvaz always called her Mrs. Ganz—perhaps Mrs. Álvaz called people by the wrong names purposely. Was Mrs. Álvaz trying to warn me that Mom was here?

"Good thing we're dressed," I told Clarissa. "Come meet my mom."

"Hi, Mom," I said, clattering down the stairs. My mom was wearing one of her usual impeccable outfits, but she looked slightly disheveled from air travel. "How was your trip? This is Clarissa." I shouldn't say girlfriend. We had only been together for half an hour. We hadn't even been on our date yet.

"Why aren't you in school? Who is this girl?"

"I just told you, her name is Clarissa."

"I have to go, anyway," Clarissa said, edging for the door. "It was nice to meet you, Mrs. Ganz."

"If that is your bicycle locked to my antique fencing, remove it immediately and never do that again," my mom said. "If there are scratches on it, I'm going to call your parents and make them pay for the damage."

"You'll have to get in line for that," Clarissa said. "Sorry, though. I didn't realize. I'll call you later, Lexie." She disappeared out the door faster than a magic trick. My mom can have that effect.

"Lexie, this house is not a love shack," my mom said. "You're supposed to be in school. Your father and I have never given you a hard time about your lesbian lifestyle, but you cannot be doing that kind of thing in this house."

"We left school because we were upset about this boy being in a car accident," I said. "He's kind of a friend—"

"Spare me your baloney," my mom said.

"This is the first day I've cut," I protested. I tried not to sound whiny or defensive. My mom hated that. Just the facts, ma'am.

"You want a medal for that? It's still September. I've really been trying to work with you, Lexie. You claim you're ready to go to college, and yet you pull this kind of garbage. I thought we were finally bonding when you expressed an interest in horseback riding. I just bought you a horse. And this is the thanks I get."

"You just bought me a horse?" I asked in disbelief. "While you were in Bermuda?" This was like the bedspread times a hundred.

"My PA took care of it. But I see now you don't really deserve it. You are such a disappointment to me."

My eyes filled with tears. I thought of my mom's essay. *Not every girl has Lexie's exuberance, love of books, tenderheartedness toward animals, and sense of justice. Even though our values are different at times, we are able to bridge that gap through my pride in her unique gifts.*

I wanted to believe that Mom bought me lavish, inappropriate gifts to express the love she seemed unable to show any other way. But then my mom said stuff like this, and it was hard to keep up that fantasy. Maybe the problem really was me. I knew my mom would have been happier with me if I were more feminine, a better student, not a lesbian, more of a preppy girl. I felt fundamentally unlovable.

I couldn't be completely unlovable, though. Clarissa seemed to like me pretty well. Thinking about Clarissa took a little of the sting away from my mother's comments.

Mrs. Álvaz was still working somewhere in the house. She probably heard the whole argument. It was seriously embarrassing. I turned and fled to my room.

CHAPTER SEVENTEEN

Clarissa

The antique fence—who knew?—was not scratched. I wasn't used to being treated like that. Did she talk to me like that because I was her daughter's queer-as-a-three-dollar-bill girlfriend? In that case it was prejudice. Or did she talk to everyone that way? In that case it was a bad personality. I understood Lexie so much better now that I had met her mom—why Lexie had such a chip on her shoulder and was obsessed with injustice.

The front wheel of my bike had to go back on again. Luckily I still had Lexie's little wrench. I got my bike back together and rode to the corner before I remembered the many calls to my phone. I checked it and turned the ringer back on. Seven missed calls from Mom, one from Dad. Two texts from each. The last one, from Mom, said, *Where are you?*

"Oh crumbs," I said. I pulled my bike over to the side of the street and called Mom.

"Clarissa, where *are* you?" Mom said. "We came to school to get you but you're not here."

"What's going on?" I started to panic. I didn't think I could take any more bad news.

"No, where are you?"

"I'm sorry, Mom. I skipped out of school. Because of Slobberin' Robert's accident. I was really upset, and everyone at school was just making it worse."

"How many times do I have to ask you? *Where are you?*"

I gave her my approximate coordinates.

"Who are you with?"

"I'm by myself now, but I was with Lexie before."

"And who is this Lexie?"

"She's, ah, my new girlfriend."

I couldn't help feeling proud. I had a girlfriend! After less than three weeks of being bisexual, I was dating a beautiful and intelligent girl.

A long silence.

"We're coming to pick you up. Don't go anywhere."

"What's going on?"

But my mom had hung up.

I took the wheel off my bike again. I waited and waited, just one block from Lexie's, until my mom pulled up in the Beemer, with Desi in the shotgun seat. My mom popped the trunk and I loaded my bike into it.

"They locked us out of our house," Desi blurted out as soon as I got into the backseat. She sounded half-terrified, half-gleeful, the way she did when something awful but exciting had happened. She had once greeted me with *Guess what? Aunt Patty died!* in that same cheerful-seeming voice. But then later she had cried and cried. I did too, but not as much.

"For real?" So my fantasy of coming home from school one day and living in a cardboard box wasn't so crazy after all.

"You weren't at school, so I get the shotgun seat," Desi said smugly.

"Uh-huh. What happened, Mom?"

"I went to Stop and Shop to pick up some stuff on sale," Mom said. "And I stopped at the tack shop in Lagrangeville to see if they would buy any of your old riding gear. But they wouldn't. Then I went home. And when I got there, the locks had been changed."

"How can that be?"

"I guess a locksmith did it. There was a little box right next to the front door, the kind where you have to enter in a combination, and inside the box is a key."

"But there are, like, four entrances to our house."

"All changed," my mom said. "You think I didn't try? And at the front door, where the box was, there was a note saying the locks had been changed because the house was foreclosed."

"But it wasn't," I said. "You got that letter about the new payment plan."

"I don't know what the hell is going on." My mom sighed. "We're going to stay at a hotel on Route 9 tonight while we figure this out."

I was momentarily overpowered by panic. The thought of spending money, any money, seemed insane when we were in so much debt, losing everything. Even buying Hostess Fruit Pies for lunch had been a struggle for me. I had been hoping Lexie would offer to pay for hers, but it hadn't occurred to her. I didn't have any faith my parents would do the sensible thing. And the banks were scamming us in the sneakiest, lowest possible way. It reminded me of an excerpt from my English book a few years ago, about a guy who was on trial but he didn't even know what for and nothing made sense.

"Couldn't we just stay with a friend?" I said. "I'm sure one of Dad's poker buddies would let us stay over. Or Mrs. Honeycutt from church. She's always saying *If you ever need anything, Sister Kirchendorfer, just call on me.*"

"Sometimes at church people say things they don't really mean, Clarissa," my mother said. Just the way her hands sat on the steering wheel had a dignity that was so timeworn and patient, I felt ashamed for doubting her. I felt a little calmer. No matter what happened, my mother's personal integrity was something we could cling to, a lifeboat to buoy us up on a raging river.

"I'd prefer to keep our troubles to ourselves for the time being," my mom said. "Although it's okay you told your friend. You should have someone to talk to. I know she meant well, with her recommendations. I'm just glad I was able to find you before you went home and, you know, saw for yourself. That we got locked out." Her voice got wobbly. "It's embarrassing enough the neighbors know what's going on. When I was trying to get into the house, Mrs. Martinez came over and said she saw them changing the locks."

"Mom, what about Skippy?" I pictured him locked in the house or at the pound.

"Skippy is staying at Doggy Day Care. I called them and they said they can keep him overnight."

More money. I pictured it all hemorrhaging away.

"Do they know he eats phones and shoes?" I asked anxiously.

"Of course they know," she said. "Try to calm down."

We did some comparison shopping at the strip of hotels on Route 9. "Is that your best rate? Do you have any special offers?" Mom kept asking. At the Marriott Courtyard, they did. We got a double. Desi seemed happy, like we were on a vacation, but I thought underneath she was very anxious. Or maybe I was just projecting. Maybe I had enough anxiety for us both.

Around six forty-five, Dad's mechanic buddy dropped him off at the hotel. Desi was absorbed in an episode of *Jessie* while the rest of us sat on the other bed and talked. I was flattered and relieved they included me in their powwow. I was afraid I would have to pretend to watch *Jessie* and eavesdrop, or that my mom would send me out on an errand, or that my parents would just go talk secretly in the car.

"Okay, here's what happened," Dad said without preamble. "I've been on the phone all day. I didn't get a lick of work done for anyone. The locks were changed by an inspector who was hired by the bank. The inspector works for a company that does this, changes the locks on foreclosed houses, called De Spinola Incorporated. He thought the house was empty."

"What do you mean, empty? All our stuff is there," I said.

"Okay, unoccupied."

"Again I say, all our stuff is in there," I said.

"Apparently a lot of people leave their belongings behind when their house is foreclosed."

Mom sniffed. "Do they leave their house spotless with a chicken defrosting on the counter?"

"Obviously, this inspector is a screwup and he made a bad call," Dad said. "Not that I ever got the bank to admit to that. But when I talked to the repo department, they did say that we should have been served an actual eviction notice before this happened, and there's no way they can change the locks if there's people still living there. The people have to be evicted first."

It seemed like the people at the bank had no idea what was going on. You expect the bad guys to be really smart, but this seemed more like fighting a big invincible machine. Not just that the bank had no heart, but it was also irrational.

"So then we talked about the letter we got about how we are now in a new payment program," my father said. "The repo department said they had no knowledge of such a letter, and the imminent default department said they had no knowledge of us being locked out. They stonewalled me for a while, but I kept talking about calling my lawyer, and after a while they started to play ball."

"We have a lawyer?" I asked. Maybe I could talk to the lawyer and tell her what Lexie had said about fraud.

"We don't, but they don't know that."

So clever, I thought. Why don't we just hire an actual lawyer?

"The upshot was this. They finally called and said locking us out had been an error."

"Yay!" I said, and Mom hugged me.

He sighed heavily. "But they also said that enrolling us in the new payment program had also been an error."

"What?" my mom said. I had read in books about people going pale, and now I saw it in real life. My mom went white to the lips. I clutched my mom's arm with an icy hand.

"So we're back in foreclosure, and the house can be placed for auction at an unspecified future time. The bank did say we can send them a package outlining our position."

I glanced over at Desi. She was rapt, although the program had given way from *Jessie* to *Good Luck Charlie*. Her lips were slightly parted in bliss as she stared at the screen. I was glad she wasn't hearing this. But she had to know sometime. She should get some warning if our parents were going to take her away to live on an ostrich farm. She was imagining being crowned homecoming queen this fall, for Christ's sake.

"When are they letting us back in?" Mom asked.

Her dad sighed. "Friday at the latest," he said.

"Friday! What's the earliest?"

"These people are very cagey. It's hard to pin them down. I hope they'll do it tomorrow."

"What are you going to tell Desi?" I asked, mouthing the

name *Desi* so it wouldn't alert her. "What does she know? When are you going to break it to her?"

"That's for your mother and me to worry about," Dad said forcefully. "Now, young lady, I hear you gave your mother a second heart attack on top of her first heart attack when she found out you had played hooky from school."

"I wasn't really playing hooky," I said. "I attended the first half of the day. So actually I just cut a few classes."

"Oh, what am I, talking to Rhonda at imminent default again? Such a technicality. You left school grounds when you should have been in class. Have you ever done this before?"

"No," I said.

"That's the truth?"

"I'm not a liar, Dad," I said. "I never lie to you guys."

"And what were you doing?"

"I was upset about Slobberin' Robert's accident and everyone at school was acting strange. So Lexie and I—"

"Who is Lexie? I never heard of her. What happened to your real friends?"

"Lexie is the girl who gave me all that advice about the mortgage, remember?"

He frowned.

"So we went to her house. And, well. We decided we're going out now."

"What does that specifically mean, going out?"

"She's my girlfriend," I said. I still felt proud, but also wilted inside because he was interrogating me. Just like they say, no one ever expects the Spanish Inquisition.

"You decided, huh? When you had a boyfriend, did we let you go over and hang out at his house when no one was home?"

They hadn't, although I had done that a few times they

didn't know about. I didn't consider that lying. It was more a sin of omission.

"I wasn't going out with her when I went over," I said, knowing my father would say I was being slippery again. "We were just friends then."

"Why do you have to have a girlfriend anyway?" my father said. "I know you kids are all into experimenting. But adults don't see things that way. You're going to make things hard on yourself, invite prejudice into your life, for no reason."

"It's not no reason," I said. "I think I'm falling in love with her."

Desi was definitely listening now, giving me the same rapt attention she'd given to *Jessie*. Love and girlfriends were more interesting than foreclosure. Mom was looking pained.

Dad threw up his hands. "I don't get it," he said. "You say you're bisexual. So you can date boys and girls. So why not just date a boy? What ever happened to that nice boy you were dating, Richard?"

I was horrified. "Robert," I said. "His name is Robert. He's the one I was telling you about, who was in a horrible accident. He's in a coma. So no, Dad, I can't date him."

I couldn't believe my father didn't know. I had told them both early this morning about Slobberin' Robert, in tears, at the start of this longest, weirdest day of my life.

My dad's expression changed to one of concern. "He's the same boy? I'm sorry, pum'kin, I didn't know."

But I got up and walked out of the hotel room, blurry tears in my eyes. I didn't have a key card, so I would have to knock when I came back. I walked aimlessly around the hallway of the hotel. I spotted a Pepsi machine. Maybe a soda would help me feel better. But no, that would mean spending a dollar fifty when we owed thousands of dollars to the bank. I leaned my head against the soda machine, listening to its humming. Tears dripped down my cheeks. I felt like I was about to crack, that I couldn't endure one more thing going wrong in my life. I resolved to spend some time with Sassy tomorrow morning at the barn before school. Even if she wasn't my horse anymore and that hurt, maybe she could make me feel better. I didn't even remember what room number we were staying in. I might as well wait here until Mom came to find me, if she ever did.

CHAPTER EIGHTEEN

Lexie

My mom called me downstairs for dinner. There's a terrible double standard in this house. If my parents don't make it home for dinner, it's no big deal. But if even one of them was there, I had to be sitting at the dinner table no matter what.

My mom was having chicken and kale, and I had a bowl of Peanut Butter Puffins with almond milk. After years of acrimony, we finally brokered a compromise where I can eat whatever I want for dinner and no one is allowed to criticize anyone else's food. You would not believe the torment that rule ended. The lights in the dining room were tastefully dimmed.

"Did you really buy me a horse?" I asked.

"Yes, I did," she said. "I still hope it will be good for you. When you have a horse, you have to take responsibility, and hopefully it will teach you about hard work."

"I'm not afraid of hard work," I said. Was that true? I had no idea. When had I ever done any hard work? Did toiling over butterflies' wings count as hard work?

"You know, a horse eats a lot," my mom said. "Don't let her eat too much. It's expensive. The woman at the stable said the horse is an easy keeper, so you don't need to feed her a lot."

I didn't have anything to say to that. Those are the two topics my mom is the most interested in, not eating too much and how much things cost.

"I bet that horse weighs nine hundred pounds, at least," my mom said. "She must have cost me something like five fifty per pound."

"Mom. Please," I said. "You're not going to eat the horse, are you?"

After that it was pretty silent around the dinner table. I spent most of my time fantasizing about Clarissa. If I learned to ride a horse, we could ride our horses together. It would be so romantic.

That whole evening, I felt strangely upbeat and positive. I was so happy I had gotten together with Clarissa. For the first time since I could remember, the world appeared to be a coherent and unbroken place. I wanted to do something really nice for Clarissa. Even though I was on cloud nine, I knew that her problems with the foreclosure were very pressing, so I wished I could cheer her up, even a little bit. I decided to bake her some vegan chocolate-chip cookies. I went into the kitchen and took out the dark chocolate chips and the flour, but then Mom started yelling at me.

"No baking, Lexie. You'll make a big mess. I don't want the temptation of a lot of cookies in the house."

"They're not for you," I said.

"No baking."

Thwarted but still cheerful, I went to my room and made Clarissa a romantic playlist on Spotify that started with the song "If You Love Someone Set Them On Fire" by the Dead Milkmen and ended with "Eau d'Bedroom Dancing" by Le Tigre. But it seemed cheesy to me, and I was dissatisfied. I wanted to give her something really special. But not something expensive and consumerist. It needed to be something that came from the heart.

I decided to make her a gift basket of items I had Dumpstered. Then she could appreciate the work I put into it, and those things could be saved from the landfill. On a previous Dumpster-diving expedition, I had found a big wicker basket with just a few strands of wicker on the handle slightly frayed. I could put her gifts in that.

"I'm going out to the drugstore to buy some necessaries," I shouted out to my mom.

"What place is open this late?" she asked.

"Just a place."

"Would you pick me up some cheek highlighter cream?" she shouted back from upstairs. "You know the kind I like."

I never buy cosmetics that have been tested on animals, like every single product my mother uses, and I wasn't actually planning to buy anything. But I called back, "Okay." I could just tell her they didn't have any, or something.

I drove to the mall. On the way I passed the MegaBank I had vandalized. I thought I caught a glimpse of the storefront covered in plywood, but really I was going by too quickly to be sure. It seemed to be another me who had done that. Sure, I still hated MegaBank, but I was too happy to go around smashing things.

You would not believe the stuff that gets thrown away, especially by stores. In a world where all our natural resources are being depleted from making more and more junk, and landfills are filling up to the brim, it makes no sense to throw out perfectly good stuff. And yet, food that is still good to eat is thrown out because it doesn't look perfect anymore, and consumer items are thrown out because of the weird caprices of capitalism. Honestly, even people who don't care about the environment should go Dumpster diving because it's like a treasure hunt, and you can find all this cool stuff for free. The first time I went Dumpster diving was with Ramone on a freegan tour of New York City where the tour guide taught us how to do it. I guess that was kind of like a date. Now I went out Dumpster diving about once a week, and I was slowly discovering which stores' garbage had a trove of magical items and which stores just had actual smelly garbage. Occasionally someone would come and chase me away, but this wasn't a risky activity.

I liked to use a grabber like old people have to pick things up off the floor. That helps me sift through the Dumpster and pull out garbage bags, so I don't have to actually dive into the Dumpster. In fact, 90 percent of the time, I do not get into the Dumpster. Gloves are key because there is some ick. I always tie up the bags again neatly after I look inside and put them back in the Dumpster. It's like camping: leave the forest as you found it. Also, if you meet other Dumpster divers, the rule is, whoever gets to the Dumpster first gets to look first. I only met another Dumpster diver once, and she was a genuine homeless person, I think, so I let her go through all the Dumpsters first.

First I went to the shopping plaza that had the health-food store. I had found amazing things there before, but I was disappointed to discover that now the Dumpster was locked. My next stop was the bagel place, but they had poured bleach over the perfectly good bagels that had been made only that morning, just to keep people like me from taking them. What a waste. But when I hit the bath-and-beauty shop, I really scored. There was a cardboard box filled with brand-new, unopened bottles of shower gel in many different scents. There were even cosmetics, including a pot of cheek highlighter for my mom. It wasn't her brand, but that was still an amazing coincidence.

That kind of thing happened all the time when I was Dumpstering. I would find exactly what I needed. It was almost enough to make me believe in a higher power. A Dumpster Goddess. Like, once I needed a new coat really bad and I let my mom buy me one. The very next night, I found a much nicer coat in the garbage on my own street. The moral is, don't buy anything, ever.

In clear plastic bags sitting next to another Dumpster were piles of belts. A bridal shop in another shopping plaza that was going out of business had bag after bag of dresses, but red paint had been poured on them. Other things I found were two cases of barbecue sauce—unfortunately not vegan, aloe vera lotions for sunburn, coffee that was just barely expired, nutritional supplements, craft magazines, a pair of jeans with minor defects, and a wooden box I thought was a humidor for storing cigars. The best thing for Clarissa was a beautiful robe still in its packaging. I thought Clarissa would love that. The coolest thing I found for myself was a neck pillow. It had some Dumpstery stains on it, but I hoped a trip through the wash would restore it to glory.

My mom was happy to get her cheek highlighter and told me it was her favorite brand. I arranged the basket for Clarissa beautifully. I knew it couldn't solve her problems, but at least she would know I was thinking about her. Then I watched *My Friend Flicka* on my computer in my room until I fell asleep. I had a muddled dream of riding horses with Clarissa. My horse was black, and hers was white. She was also wearing a white cowgirl hat. I passed the basket to her, and she was delighted with every single item in it.

CHAPTER NINETEEN

Clarissa

I arrived at the stables at six a.m. I wasn't very excited about wearing the same clothes I wore yesterday, cleaning the stalls in them, and then going to school in them. Mom had offered to buy me a change of clothes at Walmart, but I didn't want to spend the money. I was hoping I had a T-shirt in my locker at school. But before I started working, I wanted to spend some time with Sassy.

I was curry-combing Sassy under her chin—that's her favorite—when Mrs. Astin came by.

"Clarissa, Sassy has a new owner," she said, without even saying good morning or anything. "A Ms. Fialkow finalized the purchase yesterday. So I think you'd better stop doing Sassy's grooming. That's not really the kind of thing you should do for someone else's horse. We wouldn't want you to cross any boundaries, would we?"

"Would we?" I repeated, holding Sassy's bumpy little comb. Sassy stuck her big face into mine, willing me to continue currying her.

"And would you start with the petting zoo today?" Mrs. Astin continued, like she hadn't just dropped a bombshell on me. "I have a toddler birthday party here this afternoon, and I'd like the petting zoo to be fresh and clean."

Tears swam in my eyes and I couldn't see for a moment. When I blinked them away, Mrs. Astin was gone.

"Good-bye, Sassy," I told her. I had to let go of her forever now. She tossed her head and snorted. There was a lump in my throat. It seemed like my heart kept breaking by degrees, and there was always a little more sadness waiting for me. But this was the final blow. What else could happen? I put away Sassy's combs and cleaned out the petting zoo and the horse stalls. I had to constantly shake my head to clear the tears because I couldn't wipe my eyes with my filthy gloves. I also got tears all over the tack. Then I returned to my car, put my head down on the steering wheel, and cried until I was out of tears.

I was a wreck, but I had to go to school. I reapplied my makeup in the rearview mirror so I didn't look as bad. I would tell Lexie about how I had lost Sassy. I hadn't told her about it yet because it was too painful, but I resolved that now that we were dating, I would tell her.

At school I went straight to Lexie's locker. Her eyes lit up when she saw me. She was wearing a cute little black outfit that looked straight out of Hot Topic, with an incongruous man's belt.

"Hi," she said, squeezing my hand. My pointy evil-eye ring dug into my finger. I wasn't sure how much PDA was right to do at school. So I didn't kiss or hug her, which was a little ridiculous because girls hugged all the time and I had hugged her at school before. But I didn't want to give Lexie a gentle A-frame hug with three pats on the back. I wanted to squeeze her ravenously and then back her up against her locker and stuff my tongue down her throat. So I did nothing. I wondered if somehow everyone at school could see exactly how I was feeling.

"How's it going?" I asked.

"Pretty good," she said. "I have a special present for you, but it's in my car. It's too big to fit into my locker."

"That's great," I said. "I could use a special present. It's been a tough day already." I hoped against hope the special present was a clean pair of pants.

"Listen, I have some strange news," Lexie said. "My mom did this crazy thing, but I'm thinking it's probably good. Remember how I was telling you my mom buys me presents that are way off? Maybe you can help me learn to ride. My mom bought me a horse. While she was in Bermuda, no less. It's—what?"

I had gone rigid. My mind made the mental leap, and I just knew beyond a shadow of a doubt that Lexie was Sassy's new owner. Had I thought there was no greater sadness for me? Now sadness stripped me raw and left me with fury. If I could have shot fire out of my eyes that would have incinerated Lexie right there on the spot, I would have done it. It all fell into place, the way I had been utterly betrayed by someone who pretended to care about me.

"It was you," I said. "I never suspected that. It can't be a coincidence. But Mrs. Astin said it was a woman named Fialkow."

"That's my mom," Lexie said. "You knew about this?"

"No," I said. Yelled, actually. "No, I did not know! I had no way of knowing *you stole my horse*. How could you?"

"Wait, what?"

"Sassy is *my* horse! You bought my horse. You foreclosed on my horse! You are the worst girl in the entire universe. Go ahead, destroy my life. There's nothing more you can take from me!"

I yelled at her as loud as I could, but Lexie just looked stupidly alarmed. "Your horse?" she said.

"Yeah, my horse!" I could hear that my voice was harsh, like the squeaking of a rusty gate. I wished I could literally transform into the bitter, vicious Harpy I felt like, so I could actually scratch Lexie's eyes out with talons.

"My mom bought your horse? I had no idea. I've never even seen this horse yet."

Lexie was certainly processing this slowly. I hadn't realized she was so stupid. Then, of all things, she smiled.

"Hey, if someone was going to buy it, I'm glad it was my mom," she said. "Maybe she'll give it back and buy another horse. Or at least you can see the horse all the time and ride it. Or—"

"Yeah, yeah." I'd had enough of this. Maybe a few weeks ago, before all my troubles began, I would have bought into this dumb fantasy that her mom would give the horse back. But, really, the same woman who told me not to scratch her antique fence was going to give the horse back? And my parents were going to say, *Oh sure, we didn't need $4,500.* Right. And then I was supposed to be excited because Her Highness would let me ride her horse?

"Get real, Lexie," I snapped. "You act all like you are this big radical and you care about poor people. But it's all an act. You're pretending. I see right through you. Everyone knows what a total hypocrite you are. You're just a rich girl who has everything. You don't even offer to pay for your Hostess Fruit Pie. All you care about is bugs."

Lexie narrowed her eyes. "Clarissa, I don't appreciate being screamed at. We should—"

"You know what you are? You're an *enemy of the people*! I hope you have a good time with Sassy!" I yelled at the top of my lungs and walked off.

Some boys snickered, and I heard a girl say, "Lesbian drama."

"Huh, I wonder who Sassy is," a second girl said.

"She must go to another school."

The bell rang just as I slammed my books down on the desk in math. Everyone looked at me out of the sides of their eyes. I was disheveled, smelly, and full of hate. They should fear me. I sat through the whole class fuming and wondering how I could have been so stupid as to kiss Lexie Ganz and ever think she cared about me. I didn't hear one word the teacher said, and I never opened a book or looked up at the board. But perhaps he sensed that if he bothered me, I would tear his guts out, because he never called on me.

By the end of the school day, my fury had died down to a dull ache of hate for Lexie. Desi and I waited outside the school for Mom, not talking. She had called and said we were going home. I should have been happy about that, but I felt dead inside. I couldn't handle all these reversals.

Kids were streaming by all around, heading home or hanging out in clumps in the parking lot. Some boys I vaguely knew were standing nearby, flipping their skateboards up and down lazily. Mom pulled up in the Beemer. We got in, and as I slammed my door closed, the Beemer stalled, coughed, and then started again.

"It's going to be the last straw if this car dies," Desi said, echoing something Mom had said a lot lately.

"We'd have to start driving your daddy's precious Daimler," Mom said. She sounded energized and upbeat.

"So, what happened?" I asked. "Did they let us back in?"

"No, they're still giving us the runaround," Mom said. "But we're going to take matters into our own hands."

"What do you mean?" I asked.

"We played by the rules and it hasn't been working," Mom said. "I have your Dad's toolbox that he always keeps in the trunk. We're going to break back into our house."

"Whoo-ee!" said Desi. She turned around from her coveted shotgun seat and gave me a high five.

It was strange to see new locks on our door and the little key box hanging off our doorknob. We tried a bunch of different ways to open the door, but nothing worked, and it was frustrating. I ended up using a Phillips-head screwdriver to take the whole lock off the door. It took forever. Mom and Desi tried to peel away the sticker announcing an auction date, but they only scraped off little bits of it. The last screw took the longest. It was satisfying when I heard the inside of the lock thunking to the floor. I let Desi be the one to swing the door open.

It was nice to step inside our old house, although it smelled like rotten chicken. I went straight to the kitchen, the heart of the house. While Mom cleaned up the chicken and sprayed air freshener, I fingered the cherry cabinets and the Caesarstone counter top. I knew we might not be there for long, but it was good to be home.

Mom set Desi to work, writing signs in Magic Marker saying: *Owner Occupied—Go Away*. The bank had said they didn't take over the house until the owners moved out. She told me to pack up and organize the stuff I would need or want if we moved.

"I don't know what's going to happen next," she said. "We might get evicted again. We'll stay here for now, but anything you won't need in the next couple weeks but you want to keep, you should make sure it's packed up. I'm going out now to the locksmith. We have to change all these locks again or the bank people can just come back in."

Mom's attitude gave me confidence.

I changed my clothes and then slowly went through my possessions. I had packed previously, but in a haphazard, sloppy way. Now I tried to figure it out. Tank tops and winter clothes went into boxes. All my equestrian medals and trophies, into boxes. I took off the evil-eye ring Lexie had given me. How ironic, when she was so evil. I tossed it into a drawer where I kept old homework and other worthless stuff I couldn't quite get behind throwing away yet. I regarded my once highly prized ostrich egg sourly. If we were moving to Arizona, I'd see all too many of those. I left it sitting on my desk to decide about later.

By the time my mother came back, my room seemed bare. The only things remaining were what I urgently needed in the next few weeks like my clothes and my computer, and a few things I didn't care if I kept or not.

"I'm back," Mom shouted out as soon as she stepped through the front door. Desi had grown paranoid. Every time she heard a strange sound, she was convinced it was an inspector from the bank sneaking in, so we all announced our movements loudly. I heard Mom praising Desi's signs and telling her to tape them up outside. Then she came upstairs.

"Wow, your room looks different," my mom said. "Will you help Desi with her packing too?"

"Okay," I said. "But can I take the Beemer and visit Slobberin' Robert at the hospital after?"

"Sure, if you pick up Dad at the garage at five thirty," she said. "Do you want to bring Desi to the hospital? I know Robert is her pal too."

"I don't know. She might wig out. Actually, I might wig out. I'm a little freaked out already by going to the hospital and everything. Can I maybe take her next time?"

"Of course," Mom said. "I know what you mean about hospitals. When Desi was born, your dad and I spent so much time at the hospital, and then again when she had her heart surgery. It was awful."

I nodded. The story of Desi's heart surgery and how they

didn't think she was going to make it was legendary in our family. But I wasn't in the mood.

"So, is your girlfriend going to the hospital with you?" Mom asked. She had her wide-eyed *I'm trying* expression on her face.

I felt my face flush. "She's not my girlfriend."

"She's not?"

"No. It's over," I said.

"It's over? How long did you go out?"

"I don't know, a day. Less. It didn't even count."

"You seemed so...I don't know...vehement about her yesterday."

I shrugged. I liked to be more communicative with my mom, but in this case it was impossible.

My mom patted my shoulder. "It's hard to be sixteen," she said. Like that was my problem. Spending the afternoon with someone in a coma was sounding better and better.

CHAPTER TWENTY

Lexie

I couldn't even believe how Clarissa had blown up at me. It was like getting hit by an asteroid, big and hard and totally random. All that day I kept telling myself she was just upset about losing her horse and we would make up tomorrow. This whole horse thing wasn't even my idea. It was my stupid mother. I hadn't even known Clarissa's horse was for sale. How could I know when she hadn't told me? I was sure Clarissa would wake up with a cooler head and we would have a rapprochement.

But when I saw her the next day in English class, she gave me a look of pure hatred, a burning look that could incinerate a snowman. After that she ignored me. Her face looked like it was carved from ivory, it was so impassive and blank. She was pointedly looking out the window. So the teacher, Ms. Crouch, kept calling on her. But Clarissa was ready with every answer.

I started shaking, actually quivering in my seat as Ms. Crouch nattered on about the hero's journey. I tried to control my trembling hands. I was sure people were looking at me, and whispering about me and Clarissa. I wanted to appear strong.

I didn't care what people thought of me, I reminded myself sternly. They were dorks.

But I did care what Clarissa thought of me. And what Clarissa had told me was sinking in now. She had said I was a total phony, and that I was nothing but a rich girl. Talk about striking me right through the heart. My stupid parents were the ones who were rich and evil, not me. It was so unfair! Did I really deserve this callous treatment?

Yes, I did. Although I felt innocent and wronged, some part of me believed Clarissa. I was an enemy of the people and this was all my fault.

Feeling at fault made me pissed off and resentful. To make things worse, I had to start listening to Ms. Crouch because we had to go around the room and say something.

"There are seven basic plots," Ms. Crouch said, writing them on the board. "Man versus Man, Man versus Nature, Man versus Society, Man versus God, Man Caught in the Middle, Man and Woman, and Man versus Himself. I'd like everyone to tell me to which category your independent reading novel belongs."

People were mostly listing Man versus Man or Man versus Society.

The kid next to me, Ty Williams, said, "My book is Man versus Nature. That's because it's about a rugby team crashing on a snowy mountain, and then they have to eat each other. It's called *Alive*."

"My book doesn't fall into any of those categories," I said.

"It can be hard to tell at first, but every plot in the world actually falls into one of these categories," Ms. Crouch said. "What is your book and what is it about?"

"*Ammonite* by Nicola Griffith. It's about an anthropologist who goes to a planet where there's a virus that has killed all males, but humanity is somehow continuing."

"That's Man versus Nature, Lexie," Ms. Crouch explained. "The virus is the nature."

"No, but there are no men on the planet, or in the entire book," I said. This second part wasn't literally completely true, but I didn't care. "So it can't be any of the seven plots. There are tons of books that don't have these seven plots."

"I think you're willfully misunderstanding," Ms. Crouch said. "The word *man* means human."

"The word *man* doesn't mean human," I said. "We already have the word *human,* which means human. This is just totally sexist."

"It is a slightly old-fashioned term," Ms. Crouch conceded. Her eyes said, *I hate you.* "But everyone knows when you say man, it means human."

"I don't know that," I said.

"Then you will have a hard time passing English. You can substitute the word *human* for man, if you like."

But I wasn't done. "So plot number six is really Human and Woman? What's that supposed to mean? I think it really does mean Man and Woman, and that's very sexist, not to mention heterosexist."

"Man and Woman just means romance," Ms. Crouch said.

"What if it's a man and he loves a man? What if it's two women? Would you categorize that as Man and Woman?"

"Yes," Ms. Crouch said firmly. "The correct name of this plot is Man and Woman. You've had the floor long enough. Does anyone else want to share their opinions, or can we get back to our exercise?"

Clarissa waved her arm around madly.

"Yes, Clarissa?"

"Some people in this class are just trying to cause trouble," she said. "Of course we all know what they mean by man. Some people are too sensitive. They should stop trying to be difficult and picking on their teachers. Before you start criticizing other people and being difficult, you should look into your heart and see if you're really all that yourself."

Stabbed in the back! My anger all left me, and I had nothing inside but hurting.

"Thank you, Clarissa," Ms. Crouch said. "Danny, can you please tell us which plot your independent reading has?"

"Uh, I'm really not sure. It's called *Starship Troopers*, and it's about a soldier who's fighting aliens."

"Aliens are also men," Ms. Crouch said desperately. "Making it Man versus Man." If I had to assign a plot to Ms. Crouch's current situation, it would be Man Caught in the Middle.

On my drive home from school I tried to figure this mess out. For years now I had felt a sense of cosmic guilt because my mom worked for one of the worst contributors to the mortgage fiasco, both as a subprime mortgage lender and as a creator of mortgage-backed securities. My guilt had motivated me to good, I'd thought. I had done everything I could to distance myself from what my parents stood for, and to reverse the curse by making the world a better place. If my parents were going to create inequality and injustice, I was going to fight it.

But it didn't seem to be working. How could I be separate from my parents if they controlled my life and I was under their thumbs? It was my mom who had bought Sassy the horse, not me. But it didn't make any difference to Clarissa. I couldn't see how to make it right with her. Maybe it was true about punishing the children unto the fourth generation for the sins of the father, and there was no escape for me.

I felt completely crushed. When I got home, I crawled up the stairs on my hands and knees. Climbing into bed and wrapping the covers around me, I acknowledged total defeat. Clarissa had rejected me. The more I thought about it, the more I realized I was madly and unrequitedly in love with Clarissa. I couldn't wait to see her again in English class next week, even if Clarissa wouldn't look at me, even if it hurt my heart.

CHAPTER TWENTY-ONE

Clarissa

The one really good thing about the weekend was that Slobberin' Robert woke up from his coma. I talked to him a little bit, and he was definitely all there, at least as much as he ever had been. His mom got on the phone and told me the doctors said he might not be able to walk unassisted because his leg was so mangled. I was just so happy he was alive and awake, I couldn't really take that in. I figured doctors never knew what the hell was going on, so I'd just wait and see about that instead of getting all worked up over it. So I was rejoicing at first, but by Sunday I felt blue again.

On Monday I sat next to Desi on the bus on the way to school. It made me think of old times when we were kids. There were hardly any high school students on the bus because they mostly had their own wheels. So it really made me feel like we were going back in time.

"Why are you so mad at Lexie?" Desi asked me, adjusting her glasses and fluffing out her hair.

"Don't bug me about stuff you don't know anything about," I said. God, sisters. So freaking annoying. Just when I was feeling all memory lane-ish, Desi started pissing me off.

"I do know about it."

"Well, big whoop," I said. I really was turning back into a middle-school student.

"I thought she was your girlfriend," Desi said.

"She was for like ten seconds. In retrospect, I don't think that counts."

"Me and Bryan have to work at our relationship," Desi said piously.

Sometimes I just wanted to slap Desi. Did she have to be so competitive all the time? She was always arguing about who got the shotgun seat, which I did not even care about anymore, but it had been a big deal to me when I was twelve, and Desi would probably never let go of it. She started arguments about who Mom praised more. Who sat up straighter in church. And now who was better at dating.

"I want to tell you, I don't care about you being a gay lesbian," Desi said. "That's totally fine with me. I think you should love whoever you want and be who you really are."

Now I felt bad for hating on Desi. "Thanks," I said. "I'm actually bisexual."

"What's that?"

I explained.

"Oh, well that's okay with me too. You're my sister forever." She grasped my shoulders in a tight hug that actually hurt. My anger at her drained away.

"And," Desi said, pressing her advantage, "I think you should give Lexie another chance. At least talk to her."

"You are driving me crazy," I said. "You don't know how hurt I am. She's no good. She's not what she pretends to be."

"It's not her fault her mom bought Sassy," Desi said. "She didn't even know."

"Has she even apologized to me?" I asked. "How can I forgive her if she hasn't apologized?"

The school day seemed to last forever. An interminable

period of time would go by, and when I checked the time it would have been only a minute since my last look. At first I wondered if the clock in my civics classroom was broken, but when it happened every period in every classroom, I knew that wasn't the case. I was usually a really good student, but I was starting to feel sympathetic to Lexie's postal-rage attitude toward high school. There were so many important and awful things going on in my life, that going to class was just adding insult to injury. I wondered if I could drop out and work full time at Mrs. Astin's stables. And watch Lexie riding around on my horse? Maybe it was better to stay in school.

The nonexistent GSA met on Mondays after school. I decided to wait at the assigned room for just fifteen minutes, and if no one came I might still be able to catch the bus.

At minute eight, Jenna Park walked into the room.

"Hi, Clarey," she said, using her old nickname for me. "I want to join the gay-straight club."

I wasn't sure what to say to that. I wanted to be encouraging if Jenna was trying to come out or something. But discouraging if Jenna was just there to torture me.

"Great. There's no negativity allowed in the GSA, though," I said finally.

"What are you trying to say about me?" Jenna said, tossing her head so her long hair fell behind her shoulders. "You think I'm a ball of negativity?"

My Christian values required me to tell the truth, but my social values as a nice person compelled me to lie. It was no contest. "Don't be ridiculous, Jenna, of course not," I scoffed. "I'm just filling you in on the rules of the club."

"Well, I'm not gay, I just want to get that out of the way," Jenna said. "I figure, what kind of gay-straight alliance is it if there is no straight person in it?"

After the lying, it was time for the truth. "I guess I'm

surprised because I didn't think you liked me anymore. You and Pacey and Harney totally replaced me with that redhead from equestrian club."

"*I* didn't like *you* anymore?" Jenna said. "You're the one who started being all weird, like talking all the time about how bi you are, and then you quit the equestrian club and only ate lunch with your sister or the saintly Gelisano."

I smiled. I liked the name *the saintly Gelisano*. I wondered if it could replace Slobberin' Robert as his nickname. I realized I had missed Jenna, her wit and vitality. And her hair.

"How's he doing, anyway?" Jenna asked.

"He seems pretty okay," I said. "I don't know. You know he woke up from the coma, right?"

"I heard," Jenna said.

"Did you hear how he might have to use a crutch forever?" I asked. I wasn't sure if Slobberin' Robert wanted people to know this, but the words just spilled out of me.

"Yeah," Jenna said.

I didn't know what to say about this. I knew for a fact that being disabled didn't mean your life was ruined, so I didn't want to go on at great length about how terrible his future was. But there was no denying that what had happened to him was life-changingly awful. And it all seemed so pointless, but I didn't want to say that either. I could talk about how upset I was by his accident, but why make it all about me? The only thing I could think of to say that wasn't controversial was that the whole thing was sad, and that seemed like a Captain Obvious remark.

"I think it's sad," Jenna said.

"Yeah," I said, sighing.

"Do you think he's going to be different now?" Jenna asked. "I don't mean different-can't-walk. I mean different like not such a miserable drug fiend."

"I have no idea," I said.

"Is this what you do at GSA, just sit around and talk?"

"So far."

We were silent for a long time.

"This no negativity rule makes it impossible to say anything," Jenna complained.

I laughed. It didn't escape my notice that Jenna avoided all the really touchy topics, like Lexie and Sassy and my house. It seemed like she really was trying to be nice and make up with me. But she only knew how to say mean things or say nothing. Why was it so hard for Jenna to say nice things?

I decided that she couldn't really be shallow and mean even if it seemed that way. I mean, who's really like that, on the inside? All these years when we had been talking about nothing but horses, other riders, makeup, and clothes, I was secretly thinking about a lot of other things. Surely she must have been too. If she really wanted to be my friend, I was going to get to the bottom of her. I wasn't going to trust her with anything important until I had figured her out. But it was good to have friends. I needed someone to laugh with while my life was falling into pieces. And while I had no one else.

"Okay, this seems like a pretty good club," Jenna said, tossing her long hair and jumping up out of her seat. "Now, c'mon, let's go. I'll give you a ride and save you from the embarrassing cheese bus."

CHAPTER TWENTY-TWO

Lexie

I was in my room, halfheartedly editing a butterfly movie, when I got a call from an unfamiliar number.

"Hi, Lexie, it's Desi."

I would have recognized her voice anyway. She had that distinctive Down syndrome accent.

"Des, how's it going?"

"Good! I have good news for you. Slobberin' Robert is out of his coma. He woke up."

"He did? That's awesome."

I had a pang, thinking about how it was Desi calling to give me this news and not Clarissa. Clarissa had put me on her restricted list on Facebook, and I couldn't even see her posts. That was cold. Ramone and I had never put each other on our restricted lists.

"Yeah, Clarissa went to visit him over the weekend. He had just woken up. His parents were so happy," she said.

Right, Slobberin' Robert had parents. It was hard for me to remember that. I wondered what they were like.

"She said he was a little bit out of it," Desi said. "But

he was okay. He's going to be in the hospital for a long time. Because his leg is still messed up."

"Thank you for telling me this good news, Desi."

"I'm going to visit him sometime," Desi said. "I was scared to go when he was in a coma, but now I don't mind going."

"That's exactly how I feel," I said. "Maybe I'll go visit him today."

"Now there's something I want to talk about," Desi said. "It's about my campaign to be homecoming queen."

"Okay. What?"

"I think that since his accident, everyone really likes Slobberin' Robert. Before the accident he said he'd help me with my campaign. But maybe he's forgotten about it, and we need to remind him. I think if he tells people to nominate me for homecoming queen, they will, and they'll all vote for me."

"I don't know if I'll talk to him about it today if I see him," I said. "Since he just woke up from a coma and everything, he might not be thinking about that kind of stuff yet. But if it comes up, I'll definitely remind him."

"Good. Because nominations are really soon," Desi said.

"You know, though, Desi, we could do all this work and they still might not elect you," I said. "There are a lot of girls who want to be homecoming queen."

I could just picture the buckets of tears she would cry if she didn't get what she wanted. Oh God, it would be awful.

"I know," said Desi. "I'm just hopeful. If I don't get to be queen, maybe I can still be part of the court. An attendant or something, you know? Attendants don't get a crown, but they get flowers. As long as it's a real position and not something they made up just for me."

"I just don't want you to be disappointed," I said.

"But it's my dream," Desi said. "With all the bad stuff that has been happening, it's nice to have something to dream about. I really want to have a crown."

"What bad stuff?"

"You don't know? We got locked out of our house. We stayed at a hotel. But then we broke back in. And we're going to have to move. Maybe to Arizona to my uncle's ostrich farm."

"To where?" I couldn't understand what Desi was saying.

"To Arizona to my uncle's ostrich farm."

"What farm?"

"Ostrich. They're birds? But I don't want to go. I want to stay here and graduate. This is my seventh year at Parlington. I don't want to graduate from some other school, or not get to graduate at all."

"When did all this happen?"

"A couple days ago. I guess Clarissa would have told you if you were still lesbian girlfriends."

"She's mad at me. We're not talking to each other right now. Because my mom bought her horse."

"Sassy."

I was afraid Desi would be mad too. "Yeah, Sassy."

"That's not your fault," Desi said. "Clarissa is not thinking straight. If you own Sassy, you would let Clarissa ride her, right?"

"Oh, totally."

"Then she should be happy," Desi said.

"Well, she's not happy."

That was for sure.

"I have to go," Desi said. "My phone has a certain number of minutes each month, and I don't want to go over."

"Okay, Desi. Thanks for calling."

I called Sharon Hospital to check on their visiting hours, and then drove over there. It was grim and cheerless like any hospital. It was hard to find out where Slobberin' Robert was exactly. I considered just calling Clarissa and asking what room he was in, but then decided it would be an excuse. Plus she probably wouldn't answer my call anyway.

When I finally found out where the room was, I got nervous. There's something about visiting sick people that's scary. I don't know what it is. The door was closed, so I knocked. I didn't hear anything, but I opened the door anyway. Slobberin' Robert was in a bed right next to the door, and there was a curtain pulled between him and the other bed. His eyes were closed, and I briefly wondered if Desi had been wrong about him waking up out of his coma. His face was a mottled red and he had two black eyes. He had an IV coming out of his arm, and he was wearing an embarrassing hospital gown and a black knitted cap with the Islanders logo on it. His right foot was elevated and in a thick boot that seemed to be undulating, as though it had some kind of fluid moving around inside it. I could hear a snoring noise coming from the other side of the curtain, which I found unsettling.

"Um, are you awake?" I asked quietly.

His eyes snapped open. "Hey, Lexie. What's up?"

"Not much. You?"

"My leg!" he said. "That's what's up. That's a real knee-slapper, huh? Pull up a chair if you want to stay."

I did. I wasn't sure what to talk about with him.

"So, you okay?" I asked.

He made an as-you-see gesture. "They're not sure if I'm ever going to be able to bear my full weight on my leg again. I think that means I'll always use a crutch. They haven't really explained. Maybe they don't know."

"That sucks," I said. So much for being a soccer star. Also I wondered if they were concealing the full truth about how bad it was from him.

"Yeah."

We sat in uneasy silence for a little while.

"I would tell you everything that's going on in school, but I'm sure you don't really care," I said.

"You got that right," Slobberin' Robert said.

"So. Um. In what movie is the Statue of Liberty holding the torch in the wrong hand?" I asked.

Slobberin' Robert seemed to brighten a little. "*Supergirl*!"

"Correct!" I said.

"Okay, Lexie, in what movie do characters climb out of the Statue of Liberty's nose?"

"*Spaceballs*." I didn't wait for him to say I was right because I knew I was. "In what movie does a mermaid crawl out of the water onto the Statue of Liberty's island?"

"Too easy," Slobberin' Robert said. "*Splash*."

Now I felt more at ease with him. He was the same Slobberin' Robert I knew, even if he was hooked up to an IV and had a strange undulating boot.

"You want to know something weird?" Slobberin' Robert said. "I lost a little bit of my memory in the accident. Just a matter of hours. It's not, like, psychological or anything. It's just because I got a head injury. But the last thing I remember is talking to you in the parking lot. You were telling me to help Desi Kirchendorfer be homecoming queen."

"So you don't remember the accident at all?"

"Do not remember a thing," he confirmed.

"That must be weird," I said.

"I can imagine what the accident must have been like,"

Slobberin' Robert said. "I can totally see what happened. Everyone must think I am a total moron."

"Actually, everyone thinks you're a martyr," I said. "I think I even heard someone say hero. You're, like, the most popular guy in school now."

"Then they are even bigger morons than I am," Slobberin' Robert said. "I notice you didn't say what you think."

"I don't think you're a moron," I said. "I think you must have been in a bad place. I guess I'm just assuming you were drunk."

"That's a safe assumption," he agreed. "I think I must have almost died. You know how I know? My dad hasn't even said one harsh word about me wrecking the car. Totally totaled Toyota."

I knew all about how totaled the car was because they had put the car at the front of the driveway to Parlington High. And the scrolling sign that announced the temperature, the next Board of Ed meetings, and what state championships our school was in now announced Don't Drink and Drive. Like students had just never heard that, but now that we knew, it was all good. But I didn't want to tell him all that. I wanted to distract him from dwelling on his accident.

"Desi asked me to remind you to help her with her campaign," I blurted out smoothly.

"I already said I would," he said. "I told you, it's the last thing I can remember."

"Yeah, but now that you have a crook leg and were in a coma, your word means more."

"What's in it for you?" he asked. "Are you even going to the homecoming dance?"

A very shrewd question. What was in it for me?

"Not a chance," I said.

"You don't have a girlfriend?"

Should I tell him I dated Clarissa for like half an hour? Clarissa obviously hadn't mentioned it. I shook my head.

"That's too bad," he said. "Two girls together, that's like *so* hot."

"Oh whatever, Slobbo," I said. It was actually reassuring that he was the same idiot he always was. "Listen. It seems overobvious to say. But I'm glad you're okay. I'm really sorry you got in that accident."

"Thanks," he said. "I don't mind overobvious. I didn't know I'd be missed."

"In what movie does a man try to kill himself, and then an angel named Clarence shows him what the world would be like if he had never been born?"

"He doesn't try to kill himself," Slobberin' Robert said.

"He does," I said. "He jumps off a bridge." I remembered a scene where he and the angel were drying off.

"No, he doesn't. Not until the angel does. Watch it again. He's just thinking about it."

Then Slobberin' Robert's family burst in. His parents and two little sisters, all chattering and carrying packages and balloons and a stack of DVDs and a covered casserole dish that smelled delicious. It was cute because the little sisters looked just like Slobberin' Robert, same dark hair and eyes. It was weird to see that a misanthrope like Slobberin' Robert had such a normal-looking family. I couldn't even imagine how my parents would behave if I were in a terrible accident. Would my mother come visit me in the hospital if she had to take a day off from work? I introduced myself, but the Gelisanos weren't really that interested, and I couldn't really blame them. I slipped away.

When I got home I watched *It's a Wonderful Life* in the

entertainment room, which is what a normal family would call a living room. It turned out that Slobberin' Robert was right.

My dad came home in the middle of the movie. "Why are you watching that in September?" he asked. "That's a Christmas movie."

Then my mom came home. "When are you going to go meet your new horse?" she asked. "I spent good money on that animal. And it's expensive to feed."

I turned off the TV and went to watch the rest in my room on my computer. If my parents knew even a fraction of the things on my mind—well, they still wouldn't care.

The next day I cornered Heather Barrington at lunch. It was hot dog day in the cafeteria again, and the smell made me gag. Anyone who doesn't believe meat is murder just has to stand in the cafeteria and take a deep breath.

"Can I talk to you about something?" I asked, trying not to retch.

"Sure," said Heather, giving me a big smile. She was the phoniest person I had ever met, hands down, but at least you didn't ever have to worry about her being rude or mean. Her whole shtick was based on being nice to everyone, no matter whether she privately considered them dog turds.

"I wanted to talk to you about homecoming queen," I said.

"Are you hoping to be nominated?" Heather Barrington asked wide-eyed. That was about the maximum mean that Heather Barrington could get. She could pretend a remark like that was sincere.

"Not me, Desi Kirchendorfer," I said.

"Oh sure, sure," Heather said. "Clarissa's sister. Desi is so sweet. She's just such an angel. What a sweet smile she has. I feel happy every time I look at her."

How crackers was that? Desi was moderately sweet, and she had a nice smile, but it made Heather happy just to look at her? Was Desi a baby panda or something?

"Clarissa did mention to me she's hoping people will nominate Desi," Heather said. "Although, is Desi even a senior? Is she eligible? I know you have to have a certain GPA, and well, Desi…"

"She is eligible," I said firmly. Clarissa and Desi had checked into this with the administration. "She has an IEP and she's doing adapted work that may not be the same as yours, but she qualifies, and she's graduating in June, like you."

"How wonderful," Heather said, beaming. "That's so inspiring."

"Now, Heather, I know how much you care about other people and doing the right thing."

"Oh, I do."

"Of all the people I know in this school, you are the most caring. And self-sacrificing."

"Thank you," Heather said, but a worried crease had appeared on her brow.

"I think everyone would really admire you as a person if you endorsed Desi," I went on. "Think how brave you would be, how noble! Giving up your own crown so a less fortunate girl could have it."

In reality, I didn't think Desi was less fortunate, except insofar as her house was being foreclosed on. But I was happy to use Heather's stereotypes against her. I took a very realpolitik approach to the problems of life. This was something positive I got from my mother. I had mentioned this in Mom's essay, of course.

"Hmm," Heather said, but she seemed unconvinced. "You know, I'm sure it would be very rewarding for Desi to be homecoming queen. But aren't there already programs that are rewarding for people like her, where she can feel like a winner, like Special Olympics? That she could do without interfering with high school affairs?"

Interfering, my foot, I thought. But I was hell-bent on being diplomatic. If I pointed out to her how stupid she was being, she would not do what I wanted.

"Just think how bad you would look, competitively campaigning against someone who has Down syndrome. Trying to beat her into the dust," I said.

"Oh, but surely…" Heather trailed off, picturing it.

I decided it was time to wrap this up. "Which is more important to you, being prom queen or homecoming queen?"

Heather gave a tinkling laugh. "Of course, I'd be delighted to be chosen for either, or both, if the student body felt that way. You talk as if it's up to me."

"Which is more important to you, being prom queen or homecoming queen?" I repeated.

"I'd rather be prom queen, if it's a choice between one or the other."

"I am convinced that everyone in the school would choose you for prom queen if you support Desi for homecoming queen," I told her. "You'd look like a martyr. And speaking of martyrs, I went to visit Slobberin' Robert yesterday."

"Oh, how wonderful. I'm planning to visit him myself."

"Of course you are." I had better seal the deal soon, or I was going to vomit all over Heather Barrington's trendy Juicy Couture quilted satin sneakers.

"Well, guess what he told me. Apparently his last memory before the accident was saying he wanted Desi Kirchendorfer to be homecoming queen. Isn't that just so amazeballs? And he reaffirmed that when I talked to him yesterday. He said he totally endorses Desi's campaign, and whether or not he's out of the hospital in time for the dance, he hopes Desi wins the crown."

Heather looked defeated. I almost felt bad. "I'm going to think about everything you said, Lexie," Heather said. "I'll get back to you about this."

I let her go. Sometimes a mark needs to convince herself.

And indeed, Heather came to find me at my locker at the end of the school day.

"I've decided to endorse Desi Kirchendorfer for homecoming queen. I think it's the right thing to do."

I realized that Heather's eyes were full of tears. A wave of compassion swept over me. What kind of horrifying life did Heather have where she actually cared about this hollow ritual of being homecoming queen? Why was she so driven to be liked and have people's approval? What kind of thing was eating at her soul? For the first time I saw her as a tragic figure, a ghost of a person floating through the school hallways, begging people to like her. She wasn't a phony. She was a person in crisis, and no one even cared.

"You're a good person, Heather," I said, reaching out to touch Heather's shoulder. Heather didn't even flinch with gay-shyness. Perhaps she sensed on some level that this was the first genuine thing I had said to her all day because the tears welling in her eyes spilled over.

"Thank you," she mouthed with no voice and turned and walked away.

Right then and there I made a resolution. If I could connect with Heather Barrington, however tenuously, I could make a connection with anyone. Including Clarissa. If only she would hear me out, there was a chance at least that I could win her back.

CHAPTER TWENTY-THREE

Clarissa

When I woke up in the middle of the night to a strange sound, I was convinced it was some kind of bank people, breaking into the house. I had thrown back my covers and was on my feet before I was even awake. Then I took in that it was Desi standing in my doorway, wearing her Tweety Bird pajamas, saying my name.

"What's going on?" I croaked.

"There's someone singing underneath my window," Desi said.

"Really?" Maybe Desi was having a dream.

"Yes, really. But I think it's Lexie."

I felt a slow smile spreading across my face. "I think she has the wrong window," I said.

"Oh, that makes sense," said Desi. "Can I sleep in your bed? Her singing is waking me up." She climbed into my bed without waiting for an answer, grunting with the effort.

I went to Desi's room and peeked out the window. There was Lexie, gazing up. Beside her on the ground was an iPod connected to small portable speakers. Lexie was wearing her signature Carhartt jacket that made her look like a janitor, a must-have for the rich revolutionary. Lexie's hand was over her heart, like she was saying the Pledge of Allegiance, something I knew for a fact Lexie did not do.

She's a dirtbag, I tried to tell myself.

I could barely hear Lexie's voice over the music. Maybe she should have downloaded the karaoke version of whatever song it was. Finally I was able to make out some of the words, something about *breaking apart* and *pictures of you.*

Lexie had a nice voice, low and melodious. The song wound down to a close. She was looking worried now. Even from here, I could see her many rings glinting in the moonlight. I was torn. I wanted to accept her sweepingly beautiful gesture, but it seemed disloyal, as if forgiving Lexie meant that losing Sassy didn't matter.

The next song sounded vaguely familiar. But this wasn't Name That Tune, a game Desi's speech therapist used to play with her, and she got obsessed with, when we were small.

"Hi," I called down, wanting to put Lexie out of her misery.

"Hey," Lexie called, breaking off her singing.

"Give me just a minute, I'm coming down," I said.

I threw on a Parlington equestrian hoodie—it was a cool night for September—and my dad's slippers, which I had taken over. As I was heading down the stairs, I heard my mom's sleepy voice. "What's going on? Are we being evicted?"

"No, it's Lexie. The one who's not my girlfriend."

"What's her problem? It's the middle of the night," Mom said, appearing at the door of the master bedroom she shared with Dad.

"She's serenading me," I said. I didn't think Mom would be too psyched about this. "Sorry she woke you."

To my surprise, Mom laughed. "At least someone has some romance in their life," she said. "I haven't been able to sleep, so she didn't wake me. It's cold. You can invite her in.

But she's not going into your bedroom. Living room only. I'm leaving my door open, so I'll be able to hear everything. I don't want you to do anything I would be ashamed of."

I wasn't sure what exactly Mom would be ashamed of, but didn't ask. Probably lesbian sex. "Thanks, Mom. I'll be good."

I ran outside. It felt kind of magical to be outdoors in the middle of the night. "Hi," I said.

"Wait, wait," Lexie said. She had a big canvas tote bag, the kind hippies carried to the grocery store, and she rummaged in it. I hoped it wasn't going to be a freezer bag of butterfly wings. She pulled out a flowering cactus. It had spiky serrated leaves and tiny red buds blossoming all over it. She handed it to me, saying, "A symbol of my affection."

"A cactus?" I questioned. "Roses are generally thought to be more romantic."

"I know," Lexie said. "But I just have to be me, and either you like me or…well, maybe you don't. But a lot of people don't know that cut flowers contribute tons of pesticides to the environment, including DDT, and the workers who grow them are mistreated, and it's a big carbon load, shipping them to America. A potted plant is much more sustainable, and it will last for much longer."

"You're sweeping me off my feet with your rhetoric, comrade," I said.

Lexie fell to her knees. "The cactus is like me. It's prickly, but it's blooming for you. I never meant to hurt you, and I'm really sorry."

"I know—"

"Wait! I'm not done." She rummaged around in her tote bag again, still down on one knee. "I burned you a mix CD." She handed it to me. "And I got you some chocolates." She piled this on as well. It was a box with a bow saying *Alps Sweet*

Shop in brown letters. "And I got you my favorite romantic movie." This was a DVD called *Harold and Maude*, featuring a wrinkly old lady and a boy with a seventies haircut.

I thought I might cry. Everything had been so hard, and here was someone who really cared about me.

"None of this came out of the garbage," Lexie said, which mystified me. "All this is supposed to say that I realize I love you. Even if it turns out you don't like me at all, I want you to know."

"Wow," I said. "No one's ever said anything like that to me before."

"I never said it before," Lexie said, grinning crookedly.

"Okay, get up, Miss Lovestruck," I said, clutching my presents to my chest with one hand and reaching out the other to Lexie. I felt a tingle as Lexie's be-ringed hand grabbed mine. Lexie stumbled to her feet, grass stains now visible on her light blue jeans.

"Come inside. I'll make you tea," I said.

"Are your parents gonna be mad?"

"I talked to my mom already. She said you can come in as long as I don't have sex with you. And you have to sit in the living room."

Lexie blinked. "Sure, that's where I like to sit when I'm not having sex with people."

I set Lexie up on the couch with some blankets. Then I went into the kitchen and made us some tea.

"Nice slippers," Lexie told me when I brought the hot drink out to her. "Very butch."

"Thanks. They're my dad's." They were soft and fluffy on the inside, but on the outside they resembled the kind of loafers my dad had worn as long as I could remember. I settled myself onto the couch next to Lexie. Was it okay if I had my leg touching hers? Jeez, the girl had just told me she loved me, so it must be okay. I inched a little closer until there was some leg touchage. Lexie's leg was icy cold against mine. I threw the blanket over both our laps.

"How long were you out there for?" I asked.

"I dunno. I sang 'Closer to Fine' by the Indigo Girls because we heard it in the car the other day, 'Pictures of You,' and 'I Wanna Be Your Boyfriend.'"

"I only heard, like, one and a half of them. Did you know you were stationed under Desi's window?" I asked.

"Oops. At least it wasn't your parents' window."

"I'm glad you came," I said. "I don't know how much longer we're going to be here. We got locked out, by mistake supposedly, and we broke back in."

It was so good to tell someone everything that was happening instead of pretending everything was normal.

"Have you been to see a lawyer yet?" Lexie asked. I could tell from her voice that she really cared.

"I finally talked my dad into it," I said. "We're going the day after tomorrow."

"What's the deal about the ostrich farm?" she asked.

"We might go live with my uncle in Arizona. I don't want to go, and Desi doesn't want to go. I don't know if my mom wants to go or not. But my dad is kind of the boss of this family. He wears the pants, so I guess it's up to him."

With every sentence I spoke to her, I felt the distance that had grown up between us disappearing.

"You can't move. Maybe you can stay here even if they go," she said.

"Maybe. Kind of doubt it though." This was another example of Lexie's hopeful naïveté. But I figured life would toughen her up someday, like it had toughened me.

"Hey, won't your parents be mad you're out so late?" I asked.

"They won't know," Lexie said.

I tentatively laced my fingers through Lexie's under the blanket.

"So, do you forgive me?" Lexie whispered.

"Yeah, I forgive you," I said. "I kind of overreacted."

"And do you like me?" she asked.

"Yeah." I hoped Lexie wouldn't ask me if I loved her because I didn't know. I liked the romantic tone of the evening, though, and I thought it would be kind of a buzzkill to say I didn't know how I felt about her.

But Lexie didn't ask that. Maybe she was no dummy. Instead she asked, "Am I allowed to kiss you?"

"Absolutely," I said. My insides did a little somersault when she said that.

Lexie put her hand on my cheek, turned my face to her, and we kissed. As soon as our lips met, it felt so right. This was pure unadulterated lust, but a clean kind of lust where the whole lower half of me had liquefied into moonbeams. There was a tangy smell to Lexie that I couldn't get enough of. It seemed like it would never end, but it had to end, or I would start doing something that would embarrass my mother. Since I was wearing pj's, it would be all too easy for them to come off. I toned it down into cuddling and Lexie followed my lead.

"I have to get going," Lexie said.

"Okay," I said, stroking her hair. But she fell silent and didn't go anywhere.

Eventually I realized that Lexie had fallen asleep. I curled myself up around her, so we were like two spoons nestled together, and then soon I was asleep too.

CHAPTER TWENTY-FOUR

Lexie

I was driving with Clarissa down a long, bumpy dirt road. I was going to meet Sassy for the first time. Clarissa had told me to wear boots so I was wearing my non-leather Dr. Martens. I wasn't used to driving in them, and I kept stomping too hard on either the accelerator or the brake. I didn't want to tell Clarissa, but I was really nervous. Once when I was little I was led around on a tiny pony at a birthday party, but other than that, I'd had nothing to do with these animals.

We walked past a big round pen with a familiar-looking girl leading a horse. "Hi, Harney," Clarissa called, and we veered off to talk to her. The horse seemed big from a distance, and up close it only got bigger. It was an immense black animal with feet as big as dinner plates. It snorted, and I saw that its nostrils were easily each the size of my fist. Clarissa and this girl Harney were chatting, but I could not listen because I was so focused on how ginormous the horse was. It was almost furry, and its head was the longest I'd ever seen on any animal except maybe an elephant in the zoo. I was glad there was a sturdy fence between me and it. These girls were just chatting like nothing was going on, but if the horse batted that girl with its head, she would get knocked flat on the ground, and then it could trample her to death. I was glad when we left them and headed toward the barn. Butterflies were more the size I liked.

"That was the first time I told anyone you bought Sassy," Clarissa said, taking my hand. "I feel better now that I've done it. Did she look surprised to you or not? I wonder what she thinks about me now. Do you think she knows we're going out?"

"Uh-huh," I said. I hadn't even been listening to them. "Is Sassy anything like that horse?"

"Like Baxter?" Clarissa asked. "How do you mean?"

"Is she as big as that?"

"Oh no, he's a Percheron. They're exceptionally large. They're bred to be workhorses and pull wagons and stuff, but they're fun to ride too. Baxter is eighteen point two hands high, while Sassy is only fourteen point one."

That would probably have meant more to me if I knew what a hand was. We passed into the barn, which was lined with stalls. Most of them had a horse's head peeping out curiously over the door. One stall had a small pony in it, hardly bigger than Clarissa's dog Skippy, much too short to even reach the top of the stall door. It was ridiculously cute, with a sweeping mane and tail. It looked as though I could tuck it under my arm. It probably drank out of a teacup, not a trough.

"Is Sassy like that pony?" I asked.

She laughed. "You're such a card, Lexie. By the way, that's a miniature horse, not a pony."

I knew when we reached Sassy's stall because there was a homemade sign beside it with her name on it.

"This is Sassy," Clarissa said. "Hi, girl." She stroked the horse's face, and the horse made snorty noises. Sassy was brown with a white blob in the middle of her forehead and one white-stockinged foot. Luckily she was nowhere near as big as Baxter. Tentatively I touched the animal's head as she looked at me through huge eyes. Sassy's mane and body were more or less the same color, not at all like My Little Pony, the equine I was most familiar with. Up close I could see she had kind of a hairy chin. She yawned, which made her teeth and tongue stick out. She seemed less majestic and more silly that way, which put me at ease. Above her dainty ankles she had a tiny bit of hair.

"What does she eat?" I asked. "I know mares eat oats and does eat oats."

Clarissa smiled. "She eats a little bit of grain but mostly hay. She eats a ton of hay in the winter, to keep warm. But Sassy's kind of fat, so she eats less grain than most of the horses here."

"That's what my mom said," I said. "That she was a good keeper."

"Look, you don't need to worry about her food," Clarissa said. "Mrs. Astin is going to take care of that. But you do need to groom her. Let me show you her different brushes. They're hanging up in the tack area, and they're all yellow so you don't get them mixed up with anyone else's."

We went to get the brushes, and when we returned to the stall and opened the door, Sassy was crowding the entrance. "Back up," Clarissa told her, and pushed her back. She seemed fearless of this mighty creature, but I didn't know if I could do that.

Clarissa showed me what looked like a loop with a handle. "This is the shedding blade. It cuts off hair that has been shed, it doesn't pull out her hair." Then she showed me a bumpy comb that looked almost like a plastic soap dish. "This is the currycomb. You kind of exfoliate her with it. You try it."

Sassy kept walking away from me until I finally got it right. She seemed to really like it under her chin.

"After you curry her, you use this stiff brush to wipe off all the hairs. Sassy has a really wonderful coat, so if you're in a hurry you can just use this one, and she'll end up looking clean even though she's not," Clarissa said. "But I'll know. So don't do that."

"I promise," I said.

"And last is the face brush. It's more gentle. Close your eyes," Clarissa told Sassy and then brushed right over the horse's big eyes. I didn't know if I could do that either.

"And you have to clean her hooves with this," Clarissa said, tapping Sassy's knee and lifting up her marbled foot. Clarissa picked out gunk with a pointy instrument. "Ideally once a day, but that probably won't happen."

"What are those little rubber boots she's wearing?" I asked.

"Those are called bell boots. They keep her back feet from kicking her front feet. Oh, Lexie, you should know she really likes it when you scratch her withers," Clarissa said, vigorously scratching the place where Sassy's back met her mane. I figured that must be her withers.

"So let's get going teaching you to ride her," Clarissa said.

"So soon?" I squeaked. "I hardly know her. Let's do that next time."

Clarissa laughed. "This is how you'll get to know her. No, really, a horse needs to be ridden. You're lucky. Some horses need to be ridden five times a week or they go psycho. Sassy's so good you could just ride her once in a while, and she'll act just the same."

She grabbed a jingly interlacing series of straps and guided Sassy's head into it. She led Sassy out of her stall and into the hallway that cut down the center of the barn. We headed for the riding ring where we'd met the giant Percheron before.

Sassy sashayed as she walked, and I kept well clear of her. We passed a little girl leading another horse, and when the two horses passed each other, the other horse shied away nervously for a few steps. To me it looked like a narrow brush with death as the other horse could have easily squashed the little girl, but both Clarissa and the little girl acted like it was nothing. I was starting to see that horse people were made of tough stuff.

"First I'm going to lunge her," Clarissa said. "You can just stand by the fence and watch this part."

I watched as Clarissa stood in the center of the ring, holding the line attached to Sassy, and gave her commands. Keeping one ear cocked toward Clarissa and one ear listening to everything else, Sassy walked, trotted, and stopped when Clarissa told her to. Sassy was obviously very smart, and she seemed to think Clarissa was the boss. No way a butterfly would do any of those things.

Clarissa folded up the line and beckoned me over. "Okay, now you're going to ride her. I'll describe it and then I'll ride her myself for a few minutes, just so you can see what it's like, and you'll know it's perfectly safe. You don't mind if I ride her, do you?"

"Are you kidding?" I asked. My heart hurt to hear the doubt in her voice. Clarissa obviously loved this horse. "Go ahead."

Clarissa put the saddle on Sassy, adjusted it a little, and fairly sprang onto Sassy's back. They took off around the ring, looking fluid and perfect as if they were one organism. Sitting straight up in her saddle, Clarissa looked haughty and proud. I remembered how I originally thought Clarissa was a snob and wondered how I could have been so wrong.

"You see how gentle she is?" Clarissa called out, returning and dismounting.

"Uh-huh."

"You ready to give it a try?"

"I guess so," I said.

"Always wear a brain bucket," Clarissa warned me, taking the riding helmet off her own head and plopping it onto mine. "You're the same height as me, so I don't think I need to adjust the saddle. You have to approach a horse from the left. I'm going to bring her to the mounting block to make it easy for you to get on. Just climb up those stairs—you have nothing to worry about."

Clarissa coaxed me up the mounting block and cajoled me into putting one foot in the stirrup and then sliding onto Sassy's back as gently as I could. It seemed awfully high off the ground, but Sassy's back seemed broad and safe. I held the reins, and Sassy's mane too, in a death grip.

"Heels down. Toes up and in. Don't slump!" Clarissa barked. I decided she had a bit of the dominatrix in her. "Okay, I'm going to lead you around. You just try to stop staring down at your hands and look where we're going."

I gazed fixedly between Sassy's ears. It was disconcerting to feel the massive animal moving beneath me, but after a while I started to get used to it. "Can she tell I have absolutely no idea what I'm doing?" I called out.

"Of course," said Clarissa. "And you're being good about it, aren't you, Sassy? She's pretty hot and spirited if you're a good rider, but she'll just plod along for you."

Clarissa persuaded me to let go of Sassy's mane and hold the reins in a more relaxed way. She asked me to give Sassy commands—like saying Whoa! and pulling once on the reins to get her to stop, or kicking her with my heels to get her to go. It was actually kind of fun. The riding lesson didn't last too long, which helped keep it fun.

When I got off, I slid off into a heap on the ground. My legs felt like jelly, but I quickly scrambled to my feet.

"You're a natural," Clarissa told me.

"Really?" I asked.

"Eh, actually you're just okay. But keep it up and you'll be a great rider!"

We took Sassy back to her stall and brushed her more, and Clarissa showed me a special blanket I should put on Sassy if she got sweaty. I hoped I would never have to be alone with Sassy and put all this into practice myself. What if she needed the special blanket and I didn't give it to her? Would she die? I wanted to love Sassy because Clarissa did, but I was still mostly fearful of the horse.

I noticed Clarissa had gotten quiet, and then I saw her wipe a tear off her face.

"Hey, are you crying?" I asked.

"One tear isn't crying," she said. "I thought I'd never get to ride Sassy again, so I don't know what I'm so upset about."

"Listen, she's still your horse," I said.

"That's very sweet, but she's actually not," Clarissa said.

"No, I'm not kidding. There's more to ownership than a piece of paper. Property is theft, and so forth. Sassy loves you. We're going to share her. Even if, you know, someday you run off with someone else, we can still have joint custody."

"You goof," Clarissa said, swatting me with the end of the rope, but she was smiling. I kissed her.

"If you're a total lunatic, but you've gotten into the innermost fibers of my whole being, does that mean I'm in love with you?" Clarissa asked.

My heart beat faster. I tried to play it cool, so I just shrugged and said, "You tell me."

So she told me.

When the girl you love says she's in love with you, that's the best feeling ever.

CHAPTER TWENTY-FIVE

Clarissa

I was a little disappointed by the lawyer's office. I had hoped it would be grand and inspire confidence, but instead it was a little hole-in-the-wall. Stacks of folders were everywhere and the furnishings were dingy. But the lawyer herself, who was named Ms. Guerrero, was fairly impressive. She wore a beautifully tailored dark suit and said she specialized in foreclosure defense. Ms. Guerrero was a tall, dark-skinned woman with jangly earrings and a fiery look in her eyes. Her forehead was creased in concentration as she listened to Dad's history of the house.

"We bought it in 2007," he said. "My wife and I went house hunting on a whim, just as a way to spend the weekend, kind of thinking about the dream house we might be able to get someday. We thought we'd be renting for a while longer. But the agent said we would be eligible for a mortgage. We put down $48,000, which was less than ten percent of the price of the house. The loan officer said his job was to make our dreams come true."

"And did you have to provide any verification of your income?" Ms. Guerrero asked. "Like paycheck stubs or tax returns, that kind of thing."

"I didn't have to show them anything," Dad said. "They just wanted a number. So I gave a somewhat optimistic picture of my yearly income. I have a specialty business repairing classic cars, so my income changes from year to year."

"We call that a ninja loan," Ms. Guerrero said. "They're basically begging you to lie to them. In a traditional loan, they check to see if you can really afford to make the payments. And if it looks like you can't, they deny you, to keep you from buying something you can't afford. So the loan officer never explained it was an ARM?"

"A what?" Dad asked.

"An adjustable rate mortgage, Dad," I said. I wished he had done more homework for this meeting with the lawyer.

"No, he never did. But I read the agreement recently and it was in the fine print. The loan officer said it was a one-percent mortgage. Which was $1,559 per month. But that was just the starter rate, it turned out. After three months it was always at least five percent, sometimes more. The other thing is the bill listed the minimum payment first, and I always paid that amount. I didn't know there was a penalty for only paying the minimum."

"Every time he paid the minimum, it added over a thousand dollars to his loan in deferred interest," I said. "So the amount he owed kept growing and growing."

The lawyer nodded. "That's very common with these predatory loans. You were set up for failure. The second mortgage you took out was even worse. How did it come about that you took out that mortgage?"

"Someone called our home number and spoke to my wife. The person said it would be really easy to refinance and he could get the loan approved really fast. He said we'd be better off with the adjustable-rate one still, and it would more likely adjust down rather than up. It never adjusted down, though.

We ended up using the money to pay off our credit card bill, paid some medical bills for my other daughter, loaned some money to my brother who was desperate, and we bought a horse for Clarissa here."

I winced at that. If they had asked me, *Would you like us to buy you a horse with money we don't actually have?* I would have said no. But how was I supposed to know?

"I guess it was too good to be true. Maybe we borrowed more than we really needed," my dad said.

"That's what they wanted you to do," Ms. Guerrero said. "Now let's talk about what your options are. Mr. Kirchendorfer, you do have a very good case for your foreclosure being fraudulent. Everything your daughter flagged as questionable on your paperwork is indeed extremely questionable. Miss Kirchendorfer, I have trained forensic auditors who don't do as good a job as you did."

"Thanks," I said. "My girlfriend helped me. She did most of the work."

"Well, unless she is a forensic auditor, I'm very impressed by her too."

"Eeww. She's not," I assured her. "She goes to my high school."

"The lack of a promissory note is extremely problematic," Ms. Guerrero began. She became very animated as if talking about problematic mortgages was what she lived for. Her voice crackled with electricity, and her body language expressed barely contained excitement.

"What is that again?" Dad interrupted.

"That is the paper that documents the loan," Ms. Guerrero said, drumming her manicured fingers excitedly in a brisk tattoo on her crowded desk. "It proves the bank owns the loan. Your mortgage changed hands so many times—so many different banks taking it over—that somewhere along the way this very important legal document was probably lost. I can therefore argue in court that without the original note, the deed of trust is a nullity and there is no proof you, the borrower, ever incurred the debt."

"He did incur the debt, though," I said. "I don't understand."

"This is a legal game," Ms. Guerrero said. "If they're so bad at their job that they lose the note, which is just the biggest blunder you can imagine, then they don't deserve to foreclose on you. Do you know there are people who are going to pay off their mortgages in full and then discover they don't have a clean title to their own homes because of the negligence of banks and processors? So my strategy is about shifting the burden of mortgage debt back to the greedy banks who created it."

I couldn't understand all the details of what Ms. Guerrero was saying, but I got the basics, and I liked the way she was thinking. She was planning to use every stupid thing the bank had done against them. I was actually getting a little hot and bothered hearing this beautiful woman talking so intelligently. Who knew that was sexy?

"This approach could take you out of foreclosure and give you time to get back on your feet," Ms. Guerrero continued. "It has worked a number of times around the country. There was even a case in Massachusetts where a man named Antonio Ibanez, who had defaulted, was given his house back. And he no longer had to pay anyone because his promissory note had been lost and it was so unclear to what lender he legally owed money. But I have to tell you that some of the judges in New York are not receptive to this approach. Now let's consider the robo-signing."

"I know what that is, at least," Dad said. "Those forged signatures and false affidavits."

"It's really awful," Ms. Guerrero said. "There are cases of people who've been foreclosed on, even though they paid their mortgages in full, because of robo-signed documents. With this issue, I can definitely go to court and get you reimbursed for late fees and other charges you had to pay as a result of the foreclosure proceedings. It's a good tool for negotiating with the bank. I can call them and say *I know you did something illegal*. They may cut you a better deal or give you more time. But I can't guarantee that you can stay in your house."

I actually thought it was a good thing that she wasn't promising anything. It meant she was honest. If she were crooked she would just say, *Oh, I guarantee I can get you off the hook! Please sign here.*

"I also found one other thing that even Clarissa did not spot," Ms. Guerrero said, eyes widening with delight. "You were overcharged by $960 on a recordation tax, which is just a tax for the privilege of officially recording a real estate mortgage. They overcharged you, which is just out-and-out fraud. The deed they filled out is not the same one you signed."

"Awesome, so you can get our money back?" I asked. My father gave me a look that meant sit there and be quiet. I didn't see the point of going to a lawyer if we weren't allowed to ask any questions.

"I could, except the company has now gone out of business," Ms. Guerrero said. "So I'm afraid we can prove you were cheated, but I can't get you any satisfaction for it."

"Just give it to me straight," my dad said, like Ms. Guerrero was a doctor who was going to say how long he had to live. "What do you think I should do?"

"You have right on your side, but I don't know if it's worth it for you to hire me," Ms. Guerrero said. "If I were to negotiate with the bank on your behalf, that's going to cost you about $2,500. That's because even for a lawyer it can take hours of going through phone trees and talking to offshore call centers before I can speak to someone who has the power to negotiate. The last thing you need is another bill, am I right? And I can't promise we would win this. There are no guarantees. But I'm not trying to talk you out of hiring me."

"You sound like you are," I said. I wanted her to talk my dad into this because I wanted to take the bank to court.

"I just want your father to go in with his eyes open," Ms. Guerrero said. "Here's an important question for you, Mr. Kirchendorfer. Can you actually stay in this house, even if I get your foreclosure stalled or thrown out? Is there something that's going to happen to make it easier for you to make your monthly payments? Or will you still be stuck with a house you can't afford to pay off, that isn't worth as much as it was when you bought it? Are you underwater on the value of your house?"

My dad sighed but didn't answer the questions.

"In the crappy mortgage you have, the option period, in which you're allowed to pay the minimum payment every month, ends after five years," Ms. Guerrero said. "Then you're going to have to make the full payments. That's coming up soon. If you're having trouble with the minimum payment, the full one is really going to break you. Of course, I would try to renegotiate the terms for you, but as I said, I can't promise anything. Sometimes the banks are uncooperative even when it's to their own disadvantage."

My dad looked down at his hands again.

"If you do have to leave this house and be foreclosed, I

am confident I could get the bank to wipe out your debt and leave you with a good credit rating. I could make a foreclosure easier and better. But I can't do that for nothing."

"I don't think there's any way I can pay the mortgage," Dad said. "Short of a miracle." He balled his hands into fists and then rubbed them on his pants legs. "I guess I was hoping you could wave a magic wand and just make all our problems go away. But I can't pay the mortgage. I guess I deserve to be kicked out of my house. I let my family down. I'm supposed to take care of Clarissa, and my wife, and my other girl who has special needs, and I blew it." He made a strangled sound in his throat. A sob.

I didn't know where to look. I had never seen my father this vulnerable. It was horrifyingly embarrassing. All my anger toward him melted away. He had always tried to do the right thing.

"Look, I'm a lawyer, not a therapist," Ms. Guerrero said. "But I can tell you this. Don't judge yourself too harshly, Mr. Kirchendorfer. Put the blame where it belongs. What the banks were doing was criminal—they facilitated this ninja loan you got, and did not adequately explain the interest rates, and overall acted with no regard for ethics or their professional responsibilities. Your only crime was poor judgment of the situation. Your failing was being naïve. Would you blame a little old lady who gave her social security number to a con man? When I was in law school, I once bought a VCR on the street, and when I got home it turned out to be a box of bricks. I was foolish, but the guy who sold it to me was the crook."

"I guess I thought I was smarter than that," Dad said. "I never put myself in the little-old-lady category before." He cleared his throat and seemed to get himself under control. I wished so hard I could fix this for him. And I wanted him to see that it wasn't his fault, that this was happening to thousands of people.

"I don't even understand why this whole mortgage crisis happened," I said. "I mean, I get what happened to my dad and my house. But this was a countrywide thing, right?"

"Yes," Ms. Guerrero said. My dad gave me another look but I ignored him. I really wanted to know, and this was my only chance to find out.

"Couldn't the banks see the economy would collapse if they kept giving out mortgages they knew people could never repay?" I asked.

Ms. Guerrero beamed at me like I was the smartest student in the class. "Great question, Clarissa. Mortgage brokers get paid a commission, so of course they tried to encourage people to borrow the maximum amount. But the mortgage broker didn't give a—" Ms. Guerrero glanced sideways at me and coughed. "The mortgage brokers didn't care that the loans would fail because they sold their loans to companies on Wall Street. And the Wall Street companies didn't care because they could package the bad mortgages up into securities and sell them to investors, who had no idea what was going on."

"But isn't there someone important who is overseeing all this stuff?" I asked. This was all so ridiculous. If I were in charge, I wouldn't let any of this stuff happen.

"There are ratings agencies that are supposed to tell you if securities are good or not," Ms. Guerrero said. "But the ratings agencies gave these lousy securities Triple A ratings, the best grade you can get. No one knows why they did that or what they were thinking."

"Clarissa, we can't waste any more of this nice lady's time," my dad said. That was my dad all over. Ms. Guerrero was clearly a shark—a sleek, attractive, principled shark, but still a killer—and he was calling her a nice lady. Who under the age of eighty wants to be called a nice lady anyway?

Ms. Guerrero stood up and shook hands with my dad. "Mr. Kirchendorfer, let me give you my card and a folder explaining all the services I offer. You go away, think it over, and let me know if you'd like to engage me as your lawyer. This initial consultation was at no charge."

Then Ms. Guerrero gave me a bone-crunching handshake.

"If you're looking for a job, send me your résumé," she said. "I could use someone like you working in my office."

"Oh, I have a job mucking out stables," I said.

She laughed, her earrings clanking. "It's the same job, Clarissa, the same job. There are some mortgage foreclosures that need to be mucked out."

"I like being around horses," I said. "But maybe I can have two jobs."

"Mr. Kirchendorfer, with a go-getter like your daughter in the family, I think you guys will be just fine," Ms. Guerrero said, with false cheer. I was sure she could see we were totally doomed.

In the car, I stared at my father. "I think you should hire her and go to court," I said. "The bank shouldn't get away with this. You could get the house for free, like that guy in Massachusetts did."

"I'm not going to hire her," my dad said. "Listening to what she had to say was very illuminating. There's no way we can keep this house. I give up."

All I really heard him say was, "I give up."

"I want to make a fresh start. We're going to move out, and I'm going to mail the keys to the bank," Dad said.

I pictured a fat envelope stuffed with jingly keys. I wanted to ask him how we could make a fresh start when we had no money and no place to live and his credit was destroyed. I wanted to beg him to hire Ms. Guerrero, who seemed canny and capable, or to do a short sale with one of the ten million real estate agents who had approached us. But I didn't want to reproach him, or underscore what a mess we were in.

"I don't want to be one of those people who lives rent free in a house that's in foreclosure while other people are making their payments like they're supposed to," Dad said. "Barnaby, one of my clients, was talking about people who do that. Of course he had no idea about my situation."

"Dad! I know all about Barnaby. That man owns a 1962 Ferrari. He has no idea. Don't listen to what he has to say. You think he has any idea what it's like to be punked by the bank and strapped for cash?"

"My clients are the ones who are putting food on the table," Dad said. "Don't disrespect them."

Frustration welled up inside me. My dad made no sense.

"Someone else who can actually pay can move into our house," Dad said. "Why should we be keeping it off the market?"

I closed my eyes and turned my head to bury my face in the car headrest. I had gone through my life in a bubble, not realizing money could ever be a problem, until just a few weeks ago. I was beginning to suspect that my parents just were not that good with money. They were exactly the sort of people who were taken advantage of. I had been flattered my dad brought me to this meeting with the lawyer instead of my mom because I understood mortgages better than she did. But really, Mom should have been there. If I could learn about mortgages, Mom could too. And Mom should stop Dad from doing dumb things instead of going along with all his decisions.

My house, which I had lived in since I was eleven, was

going to be history. I took a deep breath and tried to think about what was really important. What my parents did with the foreclosure was not up to me. And the kind of people they were was probably not going to change. I had helped as much as I could. I could be pissed and allow the foreclosure to drive a wedge between me and my parents. Or I could accept them and love them for what was good about them. Their kindness, their integrity. In just a few years I would be in college, God willing, and then I would be in charge of my own destiny. For now, I should stand by my parents while we all had to weather this stormy crisis.

"I love you, Dad," I said. "I don't always agree with you, but I love you."

"Thanks, pum'kin," he said, chuckling. It kind of pissed me off that he didn't understand what it cost me to say that to him, but having parents was all about being pissed off at them.

We passed the Red Line Diner, and I remembered what Lexie had said about it.

"Dad, why's it called Red Line?" I asked.

"It's a driving term," Dad explained. "On your car you have a speedometer saying how fast you go, and there's another little dial called the tachometer." He pointed.

"That's the RPM thing," I said. "That says how fast the engine is turning." You can't listen to your dad talk about cars nonstop for your entire life and pick up nothing.

"Yup. There's a red line on it, which means if you go faster than that for any period of time, your engine could blow up." He made a little exploding noise. "It's the upper limit of RPMs that you can accelerate. So if you're driving your car at the red line, you're badass."

I knew Lexie was totally wrong. That crazy girl. I had a twisted sense of satisfaction.

"What are you smiling about?" Dad asked.

"Nothing." I stopped smiling. There was really no reason to smile, not even love. My family was so screwed.

"I just don't want to end up homeless or on Uncle Hal's ostrich farm," I said.

"Don't worry, we won't be homeless," he reassured me.

But that only made me worry more.

CHAPTER TWENTY-SIX

Lexie

On a Saturday morning, Clarissa called me in tears. As a matter of fact, she woke me up. I'm not an early bird.

"I left the ring in the house!" she wailed.

"What's that?"

"I left the ring you gave me! The first time we kissed, the I've-been-with-you-for-half-an-hour ring? I left it in a drawer of my desk, and I left my desk behind. When I was mad at you. And my dad brought all our keys to the bank after we moved out last weekend."

"You didn't keep any keys?" I asked.

"No. Well, our neighbor Mrs. Martinez must still have a key. She used to water our plants when we were on vacation. Will you help me break in and get my ring back?"

"Sure," I said. I had lots of rings; I could give Clarissa a different ring. We had been going out for eleven days now since I had sung under her window, so she was due for a new one. But her request was epic. Breaking and entering to get my girlfriend's ring back? This was what I was born to do. I hoped it wouldn't just be as simple as getting the key from the neighbor.

Plus, I thought maybe Clarissa just needed to say good-bye to her house one more time. I had helped the Kirchendorfers move out the weekend before and bring most of their stuff to a storage unit. It had been so hectic, Clarissa barely got a chance to look around, let alone burn sage and cry, or whatever you're supposed to do when you lose your home.

I picked Clarissa up at the Extended Stay America, and we drove to Bluebird of Happiness Court.

"Wow, someone else has a foreclosure sign," Clarissa marveled, pointing to another house on the cul-de-sac.

When we pulled up in front of Clarissa's old house, we were confounded. There was a new sign about an auction date, but the thing that really hit you in the eye was a huge Dumpster. Beside the Dumpster was a big white pickup truck with a trailer attached, backed right up to the house. The side of the trailer read Cristoforo Colombo Trash Out Company. Every door to the house was open. And burly men were walking in and out with trash bags. I saw a giant egg lying on the ground, and then a man stepped on it and crushed it.

"Oh my God, what is this?" asked Clarissa.

My heart ached for Clarissa, but I was also thinking it was a Dumpster diver's dream. So much stuff. Every item the Kirchendorfers had left behind.

A muscled, tattooed man was carrying a reclining chair out the front door as if it weighed no more than a matchstick. Bam! It went into the Dumpster.

"That was my dad's easy chair," Clarissa said. "My mom said he couldn't bring it because it's so ugly."

I got out of the car, and Clarissa followed.

"Help you girls?" the tattooed man asked. "They don't live here anymore."

"I know," Clarissa said. "It was me, I lived here. And I forgot something."

"Well," he said, stroking his stubble. "I don't know. It's not your house anymore. I don't want to let you in, in case you chain yourself to the wall or something. Why didn't you just bring it with you in the first place?"

"Because it was so small," Clarissa said. "I didn't realize. It's a ring. Lots of sentimental value. I left it in my desk drawer. My parents said we didn't have room to bring all the furniture."

The man brightened. "Was it the desk with lots of little drawers, upstairs? The pinky-white one?"

"Lilac, yes," she said. "Sort of shabby chic with a curved front?"

"I put that in the trailer for my brother's girl," he said. "Nice desk. Let's take a look."

He led us into the trailer. "So weird," Clarissa said. Here were all kinds of furniture, stacked neatly. The man heaved things out of the way like they weighed nothing and exposed a desk. "Take a look," he said.

Clarissa opened the drawer and scrabbled through some papers. "It's here," she said and held up the evil-eye ring, the stone in the center of the eye looking yellow and bright.

"Good for you," the man said. "Betcha your boyfriend would be mad if you lost that."

Clarissa winked at me.

"Thanks a lot," Clarissa said.

"Don't mention it. Good luck."

Clarissa sped back to the car, giving me the impression she didn't like seeing her house disemboweled like that.

"Shall we bounce?" I asked.

"Yes, oh please, yes," Clarissa said. She admired her ring and didn't look out the window until we had left Bluebird of Happiness Court.

"Desi says she's going to buy the house back someday,"

Clarissa said. "But that's just a stupid fantasy. Can we take Desi out for pizza with us? She's been kind of down in the dumps."

"Girls who are down in the dumps deserve everything," I said, touching Clarissa's leg. That was so her, to be upset herself but to worry about her sister.

"Dad has been hanging around the hotel room, fuming because he had to sell the Daimler, and that's not helping," Clarissa said. "Plus Skippy keeps barking, and apparently Extended Stay America has some kind of rule about how many barks your dog is allowed to do. I think we're all going bananas. I'm so glad Desi got nominated for homecoming queen the day after we moved out. That was a really good moment."

"Yeah," I said. They'd announced the top nominees who were in the running at a spirit rally before a football game. I'd gone with Clarissa and Desi, making it the first time I'd attended *either* a spirit rally or a football game. I'd managed not to vomit, and it was really nice to see Desi so excited about being a top nominee. Slobberin' Robert, in absentia, had also been voted a top nominee, which I thought was a sick joke. All last week Clarissa, Desi, and I had been feverishly baking vegan cupcakes for Desi to hand out at school, and creating a Facebook page for her campaign. After all that work, the girl had better win.

We went back to Extended Stay America and picked up Desi, then headed to Pleasant Ridge Pizza. The pizza parlor was decorated with lots of wine bottles and mirrors, and there were autumn leaves painted on the window. We sat down in a booth, and I handed over the money to Desi, who said her homework for life skills class was to order food.

"I wish my homework was buying pizza," I said after Desi went up to the counter.

"Last year in health we had to buy condoms," Clarissa said. "Did you have that class?"

"Yeah, with Ms. Nunez. I wouldn't do it. I told her lesbians don't need condoms."

"Oh, you," Clarissa said, nudging me with her foot. But then her mood changed to serious. "It makes me so mad that the bank is going to get away with it," she said. "I was just reading how MegaBank dumped lousy mortgages on the government, helped cause the mortgage crisis that created a recession, and then got billions of dollars from the government. Now they're making money hand over fist while people are still screwed. And they took my house. I wish there was something we could do."

"We could burn down the house," I suggested. "Then they wouldn't be able to sell it."

"Too dangerous," Clarissa said. "The fire might spread."

"Break the windows? Lots of graffiti? Bring down the price they get for it?"

"Yeah, that might be good," Clarissa said. "*Shame on you, MegaBank!* That kind of thing."

"I'll tell you what I should really do," I said. "Drive my mom's SUV right into it. It would ruin the house but wouldn't hurt anyone."

"Yeah, it would," Clarissa said. "It would hurt you."

"No, it wouldn't," I said. "That car is like a freakin' tank. And it has airbags. I'd be fine."

"I've had enough of stupid people I care about driving into solid objects, thanks very much," Clarissa said. "Anyway, think about a demolition crew. They don't just go around driving into things. They use wrecking balls. And heavy equipment."

"Heavy equipment like bulldozers?" I asked, thinking of the bulldozer parked in Bluebird of Happiness Court.

"Like bulldozers," Clarissa agreed, her eyes lighting up as the thought leaped from my mind to hers. Stuff like that made me think we were meant to be together. "I would totally drive a bulldozer into my old house."

"Yeah, but I should be the one to do it," I said. "I'd be better at it, no offense."

"No, if anyone is going to do it, it should be me," Desi said from behind us.

We turned. Desi was precariously balancing three plates of pizza and two cups of soda. Clarissa reached out and grabbed a slice before it hit the floor.

"It should be me because I won't get in any trouble," Desi said. "They don't put people with Down syndrome in jail."

"My pizza was supposed to be no cheese," I said.

"Oops, sorry, I forgot," Desi said.

"Des, that's a serious life skills fail," Clarissa scolded. "You should go get Lexie a different slice."

"She can go get her own slice," Desi said through a mouthful of pizza. "I'm busy eating."

"Wait, are you guys serious about this?" I asked. "The destroying the house thing?"

"Absolutely," said Desi. "It's the right thing to do."

Clarissa nodded. "Playing by the rules has gotten me nowhere. I want revenge. It's personal."

I picked up my slice and began eating it, telling myself it was Desi's fault I was eating nonvegan food. The pizza was mouthwateringly delicious, the oozy hot cheese sliding into my mouth.

"I talked to the pizza man behind the counter about my campaign," Desi said. "He was very nice. He said he's going to have a Desi For Queen special. $9.99 for an extra-large pizza with one topping."

"Wow, that's brilliant," I said.

"That's why I should drive the bulldozer," Desi said. "Brains, beauty, and pizza."

"Des, you can't be the driver," Clarissa said. "They'll never let you get your driver's license if you do something like this."

"My driving lessons aren't going very well," Desi said. "I don't think I'll ever be good enough to get a license anyway."

"If we really did this, it would have to be a secret forever," I told her. "Can you keep a secret?"

"Yes," Desi said.

"You cannot," Clarissa said disgustedly.

"I can so," Desi said.

"Like what secrets have you kept?" I asked.

"Like—" Desi shut her mouth. "You're trying to trick me! You're trying to trick me!" She shoved my shoulder, way too hard.

"You know we'd probably all get caught," I said. "We'd have to be prepared for that. Are you willing to go to jail, plus our parents will all be really pissed? You know we'll get caught."

But in a way, this would kind of be my dream. Going to prison for what I believed in, and for destroying stuff, just like Nelson Mandela! Well, maybe not just like. But what could make it clearer that I was not like my parents?

Clarissa got a wicked gleam in her eye. "They can't catch us if we do it right."

CHAPTER TWENTY-SEVEN

Clarissa

Lexie and I sat in her entertainment room, watching a DVD called *When I Grow Up I Will Be...A Heavy Equipment Operator* that we had gotten out of the library. I'd insisted that we could find out anything at the public library, including how to drive a bulldozer, and I was right.

The DVD started out with a jaunty song about different professions. "I want to drive an ambulance and go through red lights, I want to be a guitarist and play music all night," it warbled. "I want to be a conductor and take your ticket on the train, I want to be a nurse and help kids who are in pain."

"I don't know if this is going to help," Lexie said.

"No, it will," I insisted, snuggling closer to her. She was always such a Debbie Downer. "Give it a chance."

The movie explained that the blade of a dozer can move up to seventeen tons.

"That would definitely knock a hole in the house," I said.

"You can tell just by looking that driving a bulldozer is fun...but you have to be careful because it can also be dangerous," the movie cautioned.

Driving a bulldozer looked a little more complicated than I had imagined. There was no steering wheel, just a bunch of joysticks. And I wasn't sure if they were even called joysticks. It didn't look very intuitive. Plus, instead of a gas pedal and a brake, there was a decelerator.

The movie showed a bunch of different kinds of heavy equipment, mostly yellow Caterpillars. Lexie started telling me this detailed story about a strike at Caterpillar that had been cruelly broken by the heartless bosses, and then something about weaponized bulldozers that killed Palestinians. I told her to focus on learning how to drive one.

The host of the movie got to try operating a track hoe. He looked terrified, and he didn't do a very good job. The cab was hopping jerkily up and down. When the camera zoomed in, he smiled and said, "This is awesome!" but there was fear in his eyes.

"It takes a lot of practice to become a good heavy-equipment operator," explained the narrator. "Remember, kids, never approach any equipment unless a competent adult is supervising you." The peppy synthesizer music came back on.

"So, do you have that down?" I asked Lexie.

"I guess so," she said. "Maybe if I watch it a few more times." With anyone else, the lack of confidence in her voice would have worried me, but I knew Lexie could do anything.

"The thing is, how are we going to start the bulldozer without a key?" Lexie asked.

"That's just a detail," I said, dismissing her objection. "I'm sure there are a million instructions on the Internet that tell you how to hot-wire a bulldozer. You can Google anything."

Half an hour later, I had to admit that I had been wrong about that. My head was spinning at the descriptions of the different wires and which ones you stripped and paired together. The information seemed sketchy and unreliable.

"I guess we can't do it after all," Lexie said.

An idea struck me. I was thinking of my dad's garage where he had his business. There was a big corkboard with rings hanging off it, where the keys to the cars were supposed to be kept. But most of the time Dad didn't even bother to hang the keys up. He just left them in the cars.

"Let's go take a look at this bulldozer again," I said to Lexie.

We drove to Bluebird of Happiness Court one more time. It didn't smite my heart so much to see the house because I was totally focused on the bulldozer. I was glad to see Mrs. Martinez's car was gone. She was the only snoopy neighbor I was worried about. "Act like you're looking mournfully at the house," I told Lexie, "while I go check out the bulldozer all casual-like."

I sidled up to it. It was a yellow strikebreaking Cat just like in the movie, and I made a mental note of the model number. I tried to be inconspicuous as I hopped up onto the catwalk above the big tracks and opened the door. I looked inside, holding my breath.

Just as I had hoped. On the floor, under the seat, in a Styrofoam cup was the key to the ignition.

CHAPTER TWENTY-EIGHT

Lexie

I couldn't believe we were really doing it.

Clarissa and Desi were sleeping over at my house. Ostensibly Desi was there to prevent me and Clarissa from getting busy—I wasn't allowed to have Clarissa sleep over alone. And I had made sure my father was home. I had been hoping my mom would be home too, but she was away on a business trip. My father might have thought he was a chaperone, but he was actually an alibi. Earlier, while my dad was watching a loud TV show, I had surreptitiously taken our bikes out of the garage so we could get them later. And I had made sure my dad was a witness to us all wearing pajamas.

At two thirty a.m., Clarissa and I got up out of bed and dressed all in black. Desi was sleeping peacefully. She wasn't coming with us, but she was going to back up our alibi.

"Are we ready?" Clarissa whispered, and I nodded. We left the house quietly, got our bikes and helmets, and headed toward Bluebird of Happiness Court. It was several miles. A few cars passed us, but not many. As we got closer, I grew more and more nervous. This had all sounded fine and dandy on paper, but not so appealing when riding along Old Route 55 under a moon.

"Are you sure you want to damage your old home?" I asked Clarissa, bringing my bike alongside hers.

"Absolutely," she said. "I don't feel sentimental at all. I just want to stick it to the bank."

Just before we reached Bluebird of Happiness Court, we stopped and took off our helmets, put on ski masks and gloves, and then put our bike helmets back on. They were going to act as hard hats for us. As Clarissa said, always wear a brain bucket.

"Tuck your hair in," I told Clarissa. Her brown ponytail was so distinctive.

Clarissa's monstrously pretentious former house loomed into view as we pedaled onto the cul-de-sac. All the houses were dark and quiet. The good people of Bluebird of Happiness Court were snug asleep in their beds.

We dropped our bikes and ran over to the dozer. I got in first and Clarissa crammed herself in behind me. There was only one seat in the bulldozer and, more importantly, only one seat belt. Clarissa could barely fit if she crouched. There really was no room in the cab for a second person. But she had insisted we do this together, and well, sometimes we do stupid things for love. It was hard to know where to draw the line with this scheme since it was kind of stupid in the first place.

The controls were slightly different than the ones in the movie because this dozer was newer, but the basics were the same. A diagram was printed by the stick shift. I put my hand on the sticks and rehearsed how I should move them to turn left, to turn right. Where were the headlights? I finally figured out where they were. Then I adjusted the side mirror.

"We don't have all day," Clarissa hissed.

She was right. I reached under the seat for the cup with the key, and I was so nervous I knocked it over. Clarissa had to shine her flashlight under the seat so I could find the key.

All of a sudden I was sure the bulldozer didn't work. After all our planning, I would turn the key and nothing would happen. Why else would a bulldozer be left to sit for two months?

I buckled up and turned the key. To my amazement, the thousand-horsepower turbocharged diesel motor turned over and roared into life. It was incredibly loud. I was sure it was waking up everyone in the county. Plus, we should have been wearing earplugs. I quickly flipped the test switch to check the oil and water. Lights went on, which I thought was probably good. I put my foot on the decelerator. This thing was the opposite of what you expected because you stepped on it to slow down, and took your foot off to make it run.

I had to find my nerve. Were we really going to do this, or just crawl home in defeat? My heart was going ninety miles an hour.

Clarissa put her hand on my shoulder. I was sure she was going to say something like *Let's just go home* or *You don't have to do this*.

"Let's not be wimps," she said. "You got this."

My heart skipped a beat and I nodded. As if in a dream, I turned on the headlights, began pulling the controls, and took my foot off the decelerator. We started swinging the wrong way. I had absolutely no idea what I was doing.

Reaching into reserves I didn't know I had, I steeled myself. This had to go correctly and there was no room to screw up. I reminded myself that pulling back on the handle made the tracks turn right and pushing forward was left. I positioned us the right way, lifted up the stick, and we went forward. We were headed straight for the side of the house, where the living room was. Now I ground the gear into third, and we sped up. Bulldozers don't exactly fly along, but it seemed pretty fast to me.

Every instinct in my body told me to slow down, but I removed my foot from the pedal completely to open her up. With my other hand I used the third control to lift the blade to eye level, to shield our windshield from the collision. I could still see around the blade a little. My body was actually shivering in fear, so it was a good thing I didn't have to do any fancy steering. The wall rushed up to us. Clarissa was screaming. The blade of the bulldozer hit the wall.

At the moment of impact, I couldn't help stepping on the pedal a little as everything seemed to explode in a sickening crunch. My whole body was slammed forward with the greatest force. Clarissa was tossed into me like a doll, and I could feel my teeth rattle. I saw the blade tear a huge jagged hole in the wall. The world was a mass of noise and white bits flying everywhere. Now we were inside the house. I slowed down further. Little clouds of fiberglass insulation, like puffs of dandelions, were everywhere, making it hard for me to see.

We crashed through a second wall and bumped into something else, and I stopped the dozer. I had the presence of mind to lower the blade so I could see better. There were pieces of drywall littering the windshield. I couldn't help but notice Clarissa was cursing a blue streak.

"Are you okay?" I screamed.

"I'm fine," shouted Clarissa. Her bike helmet was dented, but she was grinning a lunatic smile.

There was an ominous creaking sound.

"I think the ceiling is going to collapse," Clarissa said. "Let's get out of here."

I wondered, too late, if the dozer had windshield wipers and, if so, how to turn them on. The exhaust coming out of the stack was filling the room too. My eyes started to get used to the white stuff all over the windshield, and I could see we were in the kitchen, and we had just knocked over the island. My headlights illuminated the cherry cabinets. I tried to look in the side mirror to see behind us, but it had been lopped off.

I threw the dozer into reverse, and it beeped madly as I tried to back up while turning. Reverse seemed faster even than third gear. The dozer leaped backward and bumped into a wall. The house shook. The entrance hole we had crashed from the living room to the kitchen was to our right. It would be hard to maneuver back out that way again. I went forward, bumped the island again, then threw it in reverse. We crashed backward through the wall in a shower of dust. The creaking sound got louder. Now we were in the large, empty living room, perfect for turning around in. I realized we were almost out, got rattled, and steered the dozer in the wrong direction. I had no idea what my hands were doing and everything happened so fast. We plowed into the staircase. The blade snapped the newel-post of the staircase like it was a twig. I stopped the dozer and took a deep breath.

"Hurry up and get us out of here!" Clarissa screamed. "Should we just get out and run?"

"No, I can do it!" I circled the spacious living room, white dust sprinkling from the ceiling, until I was positioned right in front of the hole. Sparky electrical cables dangled from the wall into the void we had smashed. Driving over all the debris like it was nothing, we went outside.

I didn't even bother to turn the bulldozer off, just unbuckled my seat belt and tumbled out the door. My foot slipped off the little catwalk and I landed on the vibrating track, then fell to the ground. When I scrambled to my feet, Clarissa was ahead of me, already racing for her bike. I was close on her heels. I glanced back once at the silhouette of Clarissa's old house. It had a huge gaping hole, and the whole structure seemed to be sagging.

Clarissa did that thing where she jumped onto her bike while running, but I wasn't graceful enough for that. We barreled down the cul-de-sac. Now there were plenty of lights on in the houses, and I was sure each and every person was dialing 911. Turning onto Route 216, we stood up on our pedals and rode as fast as we could.

My face stung where my head had collided with Clarissa's. We had only been biking for about a quarter of a mile when we heard a car engine coming. We plowed straight into the shrubbery on the side of the road and waited. A cop car sped by. I held my breath, as if the police could hear us. As soon as it was gone, we peeled off our ski masks, left them in the bushes, and got back on the road. We turned as soon as we could onto Old Route 55.

Clarissa whooped. "I can't believe we did it!"

I grinned, but I couldn't celebrate until we were safe back at my house. All of a sudden all my adrenaline was gone, and I was almost too tired to pedal. Our flashlights bobbed in the dark. I felt like I was in the movie *E.T.*, only my bike wouldn't fly.

We left our bikes in the yard, hidden behind a hydrangea bush. Clarissa made us change back into our pj's before we raided the fridge. Desi was wide awake waiting for us, and Clarissa hurriedly whispered to her what a success our mission had been. Back in bed, hugging a box of Orgran animal crackers, I finally relaxed.

"I can't believe we got away with it," I whispered.

Desi and Clarissa started singing some Taylor Swift song, but I didn't know the words. They both had nice voices, similar in pitch, but Desi was always a few words behind and rushing to catch up.

Just then, the doorbell began to ring insistently. We glanced at each other, fear in our eyes.

I waited to hear my father go down and answer the door. Then I crept down the stairs to listen.

"I'm Officer Farley. Does a Lexie Ganz reside here?" a deep male voice asked.

My father had turned on the light, so I could see him clearly, but the figure on the porch was just a silhouette to me.

"What's this about?"

"Police investigation. Are you the father of Lexie Ganz?"

"I'm sorry, Officer, but I'd really need to know why this is something you need to know before I help you. What's going on?"

Way to go, Dad, I thought fearfully. Know your rights.

"Mr. Ganz, we have reason to believe your daughter may have been involved in some kind of criminal activity. If you're not going to help us, we'll have to assume she's not here."

"Yes, she is here," my dad said. "She's sleeping. Obviously."

"Can we speak to her?"

"Absolutely not," Dad said. "Look, I'm a friend to the police. I donate to the Police Benevolent Association. I was a chairman of the PAL gala ball in 2011."

"We treat everyone the same when a crime has been committed," the cop said. "I really need to speak to your daughter."

"But my daughter is a sensitive girl, and you're not going to speak to her right now, in the middle of the night."

I was so proud of my father. He was actually protecting me.

"Is there anyone else staying here?" the cop asked.

"I'm sorry, but I can't answer any more questions," my father said. "Good night."

"We spoke to a Mr. and Mrs. Kirchendorfer, whose

daughter is also someone we need to speak to. They said she's here, that both their two children are here. Is this true?"

"I'm sorry, Officer." My dad began to close the door and the officer stuck his foot in it.

"May I come in?" the cop asked.

"No, you may not come in."

I could hear Clarissa and Desi whispering and creeping down the stairs behind me. It sounded like Clarissa was coaching Desi on our story.

"Then I *will* return later with a warrant. It's easier if you just let me in now."

"I'd prefer to wait until you have a warrant—if you even want to go to all that trouble."

"It is a lot of trouble to get a warrant. I might not have to if I knew for a fact that your daughter and the other girl are here. How about if they just come to the door? They don't have to say anything. Then I'll go."

My father glanced behind him, the first sign he had made showing he knew I was there. "Officer, let me go see if the girls are awake and can come to the door. It's the middle of the night after all. I'm going to close the door now, and you just wait right here. I'll be back. But I can't close the door if your foot is there. I don't want to bump your foot. Can you please move your foot, sir?"

I didn't think the cop was going to move his foot, but he did. My dad shut the door gently, then chained and locked it. He turned and his eyes blazed out at me.

"I don't know what you did," he said, "but I can guarantee you are going to be severely punished for this. But you'll be punished by me, not by the cops."

The other two girls trooped down the stairs. Clarissa was clutching her stomach in a stagy way.

"I don't believe this guy is just going to leave if he sees

you," my dad said. "We have no legal obligation to talk to him or let him in. Unless he goes and gets a warrant, and then we have to let him in. So what do you want to do? Do you think it would help if he knows you're home?"

"I didn't do anything, Dad," I lied.

"Have you girls really been here all night?" my dad whispered.

"We certainly have," Clarissa said. "I've been throwing up all night. I think I had food poisoning. You probably heard me walking to the bathroom and retching, over and over again."

My dad stared at us for a long time.

"I certainly did," he finally said. "It woke me up."

Had they all lost their minds? Then I realized what was going on. They were constructing an alibi.

"I think you might have even come upstairs at one point to see how I was doing," Clarissa noted, her voice rising, like she was asking a question.

"I certainly did," he repeated. "Although I'm not sure what time that was. I wasn't paying attention."

"Well, me neither really," Clarissa said. "I was too busy throwing up."

The doorbell rang again.

I nodded at my dad, and he opened the door. This time he flipped on the porch light, and the police officer was illuminated. Clarissa, Desi, and I huddled together at my dad's side. Dad led us outside onto the porch and shut the door again, I supposed to prevent the cop from barging in and searching our home.

"Here they are," Dad said.

The officer asked us for our IDs, which we had to go and get, and then asked me and Clarissa a lot of questions about where we'd been all night. He asked Clarissa about the house, the foreclosure, but he never said what had happened to the house or why he was questioning us. We both said that Clarissa had been throwing up all night.

"Can you corroborate that they've been here all night?" the officer asked my father.

"Of course I can," he said. "Clarissa was vomiting so loudly it woke me up."

"I'm sorry," Clarissa said.

He patted her shoulder. "Not your fault," he said. "Although maybe you shouldn't eat with such gusto."

This was so weird.

"What's that gash on the side of your face from?" the cop wanted to know.

"I banged my head against the toilet," Clarissa said.

The officer turned to Desi. "So what were you doing all night, Desiree?" he asked.

Oh, now we are well and royally screwed, I thought. Desi was standing in an awkward hunched position, her head craning forward, as uncomfortable-looking as a girl could be.

"Sleeping mostly," she said. "But I woke up a lot."

"And why is that?"

"My sister, she kept puking. She kept running to the bathroom. It was loud. And I was worried about her."

Clarissa suddenly bolted off the porch and leaned over the flower bed. She vomited copiously.

"Just like that," said Desi, flashing a smile.

"Can I go inside now?" Clarissa asked pitifully. "I want to call my mom."

The cop nodded, and Clarissa went inside.

"And was Lexie there too? Or did she leave?" the cop asked Desi.

"Yes, she kept waking up too, to see if Clarissa was all

right. We were all sleeping in the same room because it was a slumber party. Did you know Clarissa and Lexie are lesbian girlfriends?"

"You don't have to get into that," my dad said. The cop made a strangled sound.

"Is everything all right? I'm scared," Desi said, blinking up at the cop.

"Don't be scared," he told her. "You're not accused of anything."

"Don't you know that people with Down syndrome are incapable of lying?" my dad said.

I thought that was going too far, but the officer flipped his book closed and said, "I believe it, sir. They're like angels from heaven. Have a good night."

We all went inside quickly, before the cop could change his mind. Desi ran up the stairs after Clarissa, and I was left all alone with my father.

"Lexie, what did you do?" he asked grimly.

"Um, would you believe nothing?"

"No, I would not. I'm going to tell your mother about this first thing in the morning. I'm going to call her, and she'll know what the hell to do with you. I'm at a loss. We'll discuss this in the morning."

I went upstairs. Desi and Clarissa were laughing and hugging.

"You guys were amazing," I said. "Des, you played that cop like an ocarina! That was brilliant. And Clarissa, how did you throw up like that?"

"As scared as I was, it was not hard," Clarissa said. "Mind over matter."

"We did it!" Desi said. "We are good actresses. Maybe we should all try out for the play this year."

"Your dad was so cool," Clarissa said.

We talked deliriously for another few minutes, then Clarissa's phone rang. I heard her talking to her mom on the phone, but my tiredness caught up with me and I fell asleep.

Clarissa's mom came for them at the crack of dawn, she was so worried, but I slept until almost eleven. When I finally went downstairs, my dad was sitting in the entertainment room poking at his iPad. When he looked up, his face was like a thundercloud.

"Was this you?" he asked, turning the screen around and bringing the *Poughkeepsie Journal* app to the front.

Foreclosed Home Destroyed by Dozers in the Night, the headline read. *Could anarchists be to blame?* was the subheading.

"Umm," I said. I wanted to lie, but he obviously knew.

"The less I know, the better," he said. "You are grounded, until forever. What is wrong with you? You're probably defective. I'm sending you to a shrink, and if he says you should be locked up, I won't even blink before I do it. And I am sending you to military school. On second thought, I'm not. They would probably teach you to make bombs or something. I told your mother she has to stop going on business trips so she can keep an eye on you."

"I'm sorry, Dad," I said, but he was not done.

"You want to know what's really hilarious? I got an e-mail this morning from Simon's Rock College saying you had been accepted into their January class. You didn't even have my permission to apply! You'll be lucky if I let you leave the house in January, let alone go to college."

"Dad," I interrupted. "I really appreciate your helping me out last night."

"What else do you expect?" he said irritably. "Do you think that would make me look good? It would be a big scandal."

"It's not just that though, right?" I pressed him. "You

covered up for me because you love me." My voice broke a little on the word *love*. I wasn't even embarrassed because I was sure I was right.

"I don't want to see my own kid go to jail," he said. "There's such a thing as loyalty, you know. It would be like wearing a wire and turning in the traders I worked with at Golden Slacks."

I sniffed a little, I was so moved.

"Cut it out," he said. "Don't cry. I'm going to talk to Sheriff Anderson. We're golf buddies. He'll make sure nothing more comes of this."

I smiled happily. My dad loves me, I thought to myself. He doesn't want to see me go to jail.

Chapter Twenty-nine

Clarissa

"Wow, it looks amazing!" I said, as we walked through a balloon arch anchored to two cardboard pineapples. The gym had been decorated in a Hawaiian luau theme. A tropical banner featuring an exotic bird told us to *Party in Paradise.* Mylar balloons in the shape of palm trees floated in the air. There was some kind of sparkly blue stuff that was probably supposed to be a waterfall hanging from one wall, while another wall sported a sunset. The basketball nets had been covered with grass skirts, and the DJ's stage was next to a big treasure chest. All the chaperones were wearing Hawaiian shirts and had plastic flower garlands around their necks.

"It still smells awful," Lexie said.

"You hush," I said, grabbing her hand. "The decorating committee worked all night putting this stuff up. Jenna had to drink Red Bull and take NoDoz."

"I'll be quiet," Lexie promised. "I should be voted off the island for criticizing it. I love celebrating the exploitation of a native culture. You know there are almost no native birds in Hawaii, right, because of human impact?" She pointed to the bird on the *Party in Paradise* banner.

"Hush," I repeated.

I spotted my parents at the punch station, but they had promised not to bother me. I wasn't planning to acknowledge them unless maybe they were serving me some punch, when it would be a little weird not to say anything. My dad looked moderately studly in his Hawaiian shirt. He was in a really good mood today because someone had run into our Beemer while it was parked on the street in front of Mrs. Honeycutt's, and we were going to get a bunch of insurance money. He said his financial plan for the coming year was to turn the Beemer around and expose its other side.

I felt nervous walking into the gym holding Lexie's hand. I had never done anything so visibly queer before. But it would be über depressing to drag my girlfriend to homecoming and then be too chicken to hold hands. I figured there was a better chance of hearing catty comments in the girls' bathroom or on Facebook than there was of some overt homophobia on the dance floor.

No one acted like it was a big deal. Some girl from equestrian club smiled at me and said, "I hope Desi wins." It seemed like the whole queer thing was upstaged by Desi, who was big news.

"Did you vote for her?" I demanded. Maybe everyone was smiling and saying they hoped Desi would win, but they had all actually voted for someone else. The voting had been done online, and everyone had a secret ballot.

"Umm, I actually forgot to vote," the girl said. "But I hope she wins."

"You forgot?" I said. "Where's your school spirit? Didn't you get one of Desi's cupcakes? They were delicious, even if they were vegan."

"Leave her alone," Lexie said, jerking me away from the girl.

I saw Mr. Viscount, the vice principal, glowering at us. It wasn't an antigay glower, it was a *You brought cops to my school* glower. I had never been on Mr. Viscount's radar before, but Lexie and I had been called into the office separately and been questioned by the cops. We stuck to our story, and no one questioned Desi, so we were okay, but now Viscount hated us. I just really hoped Desi never slipped up and told our parents. They were the only people who would believe what Desi could tell them. Our parents were so innocent they had never connected all the dots, and they would be shocked.

"Let's go get our pictures taken," I said.

We got in line at the photo backdrop. Couples, and sometimes groups of friends, stood next to giant Easter Island statue cutouts and had their pictures snapped by a professional photographer.

"Don't say anything about how Easter Island is not Hawaii," I warned Lexie. "You try decorating a gym on a small budget. I bet it's hard."

"Did you know Easter Island used to be covered by tons of trees, but the islanders chopped them all down? And then their soil got eroded and the climate changed and everything went downhill for them. So when the first white people showed up, they were all like, Who put up these amazing statues? It couldn't possibly be these raggedy people who live here now."

The photographer gestured to us. "Your turn."

I positioned myself slightly in front of Lexie. I was relieved Lexie knew the traditional photo stance and put her hands on my waist. I knew we looked great together. I was wearing a strapless pink gown with a puffy skirt with an appliquéd flower on it. The skirt spun when I turned. I had been really worried about the dress because I was broke. Lexie had presented me with that dress and another dress that was kind of tacky. Mrs.

Honeycutt, whose basement we were staying in temporarily, had altered this one to fit me better. Lexie swore she hadn't spent a dime on the dresses, but she wouldn't tell me where they came from. My only concern was that my summer tan line hadn't faded completely, and I thought the bathing suit lines on my shoulders looked stupid. But I was pretty sure my hair looked amazing.

Lexie looked wonderful. She was wearing a navy tuxedo with satin lapels and barrel sleeves. It looked great against her pale skin, and she had styled her hair into a fauxhawk.

Lexie wore one other fashion accessory, which couldn't be seen under the pant leg of her tux. This was an ankle bracelet containing a GPS device. Her parents had made her wear this following the bulldozer incident, so they could keep track of where Lexie was at all times. There was another one in her car that even kept track of whether she was going over the speed limit. I thought that normal parents would just spend more time with their kid if they were so worried about her instead of buying all these devices, but I guess her parents didn't roll like that. Lexie hadn't figured out a way to hack either of the GPS devices yet. She didn't mind seeing the shrink. Lexie said the shrink was really nice, but she didn't like being treated like a prisoner.

"Smile!" The camera flashed. The photographer's assistant beckoned us over to the screen to see what the picture looked like. It was perfect. I was afraid Lexie would be pouting, but she just looked sultry.

"I look so skinny. We'll take two of these," I told the photographer's assistant. "If I have to move to Arizona, we'll need something to remember each other by."

"Let's not think about that," said Lexie, squeezing my hand.

I had been having nightmares about moving to Arizona and starting a new life of cleaning ostrich poop. I knew Lexie was worried about it too. But we never talked about it because it was just too depressing.

We drifted over to the dance floor. But no sooner had we begun dancing when the DJ, who was on a small stage, cut the music and handed the microphone to the senior class president.

"Ladies and gentlemen," she announced. "Thank you for coming to the homecoming dance, and for all your spirit during homecoming week. Now it's time to announce the homecoming court."

"Our prince is...Ty Williams."

Ty Williams raced up to the stage, grinning. Ty is this dude bro type who always wears cargo pants and a shirt with a popped collar. He goes out with Heather Barrington, works at Planet Wings after school, and for whatever reason is extremely well-liked. Today he was in a suit, but he still chose to pop the collar. The class president gave Ty a sash, and then continued, "Our homecoming king is...Robert Gelisano!"

Everyone broke into rapturous applause except for some people in the corner who obviously didn't have any school spirit.

"You owe me five dollars," I told Lexie.

"Boy, is he going to be pissed," she commented. We both clapped, though.

Everyone kept clapping and looking around for Slobberin' Robert. Eventually it became clear he was one of the people lurking in the corner, and he walked slowly over to the stage on his crutches. He had been back at school for four days, and he really hadn't wanted to come to this dance. He kept saying he wanted to order the Desi For Queen pizza pie special with ham and watch *Highlander* instead. But I leaned on him pretty hard to show up, and he ended up taking Pacey's little sister for his date. Slobberin' Robert was given a crown. He looked the opposite of thrilled.

"And now for the ladies."

My heart was pounding. I tried to look cas, but I hadn't been this freaked out since we ran over my house with a bulldozer. I hoped I wouldn't puke, as classic a school dance experience as that would be. I tried to catch Desi's eyes, but she was standing with some other special-ed girls not looking my way. She was looking calm and expectant. Why was I the one who was a nervous wreck?

"Our two homecoming attendants are Haileigh Askegaard and Tyreshia Harris."

Applause. The two girls came to the stage and accepted their bouquets. Oh God, that meant either Desi was the winner or she got nothing. I glanced at Lexie. She looked awfully anxious herself and put her arm around my waist.

"And our homecoming queen is…" She paused like it was the Oscars. "Desiree Kirchendorfer!"

The gym exploded into wild cheers and whistles. Everyone in the gym began chanting *Desi! Desi!* When school started this fall, hardly anyone knew her name, and now everyone was shouting it. People stamped their feet so much I could feel the vibrations through my high heels. My heart was so full I felt fluttery. Lexie squeezed me in a crushing hug.

With a demure smile, Desi walked up to the podium with mincing steps. She was wearing a powder-blue dress that came down to her knees, with one ruffled sleeve and one thin strap. Roses and leaves were embroidered on the skirt. My family had been going crazy trying to find a dress that would fit her, look nice, and we could afford. Finally Jenna Park had come up with this one, which someone in her family had worn as a bridesmaid dress. Desi looked terrific. I had spent an hour at least on her makeup.

The class president placed a glittering tiara on Desi's head. Desi beamed. I was pretty sure we would never be able to get that tiara off. She would sleep with it, bathe with it, and try to wear it under her riding helmet.

"Desiree is a very special student," the class president said. "She has taught us that true beauty is within all of us."

"What the hell is that supposed to mean?" Lexie whispered in my ear. "Desi looks beautiful, *regular* beautiful. Why is it within?"

"Shhh," I said. Lexie was very literal minded. She listened to the actual words people said, and then she would try to argue with them. The content of the class president's remark was clear to me, even if the actual words didn't make a ton of sense. She was trying to say that Desi was awesomesauce.

It looked like the class president planned to say more, but Desi grabbed the microphone. I had heard muttering coming from the bathroom all week as Desi practiced her speech in the mirror, but I had never actually heard the speech. I had decided listening to it would be bad luck. We had spent all our time warning her she might not win.

"I am so surprised and amazed you chose me for homecoming queen," Desi said slowly and clearly. "I just can't believe it. Any of the nominees would be a great homecoming queen. This is one of the most amazing experiences I ever had. I just want to say thank you, and all your dreams can come true. Special thanks to my mom and dad and my sister Clarissa and her lesbian girlfriend Lexie and my boyfriend Bryan and Heather Barrington for helping me. I wish for world peace. Other than that, my next dream is to graduate in June right here from Parlington High School." Then she smiled and passed the microphone back.

People cheered and clapped again, and they lined up to hug Desi as she came off the stage. Lexie and I stood watching Desi being thronged by admirers.

"I am really happy for her," Lexie said. "She seriously deserves this. And I don't mean to sound like a naysayer, but it seems like everyone is smugly patting themselves on the back, like being homecoming queen is something they extended from on high down to a lowly girl. So once again, it's all about them, how nice they are, not really about Desi."

"It doesn't matter," I said absently, watching the scene. "They don't even know Desi. They don't know her like we do. We know the real deal. Anyway, I thought I told you—no negativity at the dance."

"If you only knew how hard I'm working just to be here at all and not run screaming—"

I pinched her butt. "Pipe down. If you're good, I will reward you later, after the dance. And I don't mean vegan ice cream."

Lexie's mouth hung open. "Really?"

Then my parents came over and hugged me. I was pretty sure they hadn't seen me pinching Lexie's ass. I wasn't even mad they had broken the rules about not acknowledging me at the dance. Lexie tactfully faded away so we could have our family moment. My mom looked radiant, and I couldn't remember when she had last looked so happy. My dad had tears in his eyes. He was turning into a regular crybaby, he cried so much lately.

"Look, there are so many kids congratulating Desi we couldn't even get close to her," Mom marveled.

"Hope she'll remember her old parents now that she's queen," Dad joked.

"Did you hear what she said about wanting to graduate

from Parlington?" Mom said. "Let's start looking for an apartment right here in the area."

"Are you for serious?" I squealed. But I knew it wasn't up to Mom. Mom hardly ever expressed an opinion about what the whole family should do, only about Desi.

"I am," she said. "Tom, what do you think? I really don't want to move to Arizona."

"You don't?" Dad looked surprised.

"No. I think we can make it here. You have your job here, and Clarissa already has two jobs here. I'm thinking of expanding my business to include collectibles highlighting other disabilities and conditions. And I can send out my paraphernalia from anywhere. Let's not make the kids change schools in the middle of the year and leave both their sweethearts behind. They really appreciate Desi here at this school—and Love Bug too, of course. It would be great if they could both graduate from Parlington High. I know you want to make a fresh start, but what if we go all the way to Arizona and you can't get a job?"

"You're my clever gal," Dad said. "If that's what you think. My brother did send me a text message that a lot of his ostriches have died. I don't think things are going so well out there. I bet there are some nice two-bedroom apartments for rent in Poughkeepsie."

Desi barreled over to us and hugged us all. Her petite features were aglow. But before I could even say anything to her, the music started up and the DJ said in a voice that sounded like he was eating peanut butter, "Ladies and gentlemen, it's our first sloooow dance."

A slow Jennifer Hudson song came on. Desi grabbed her boyfriend Bryan. Desi and Bryan pressed up against each other, glasses glinting.

Lexie reached out her hand and I took it. I draped myself over her, enjoying the feeling of her curves, and rested my cheek against Lexie's soft one. I hoped I wouldn't leave a trail of makeup.

"Guess what?" I said. "We're staying in town. No Arizona for me."

Lexie squeezed me so hard I could hardly breathe. "That is straight-up amazing! I don't mind about not going to Simon's Rock as long as you're here."

I whispered into Lexie's ear, "I love you." Lexie snuggled up closer to me.

I couldn't believe that all my life I would have to remember this crappy song. I would be an old lady, buying food in the supermarket, and this song would come on. I would stop in the aisle and say, *Ah. That was my first dance with my first girlfriend.* Or maybe I would be married to Lexie, and my eyes would mist over at these terrible lyrics. Between the relief at not having to move, the joy for Desi, and dancing with Lexie, I felt lighter than air. I would get to move out of Mrs. Honeycutt's basement, and I was not incarcerated for the bulldozer incident.

Lexie's pointy rings were digging into my back, but I liked it. I had started out hating her, but now she was my perfect girlfriend.

Epilogue

Lexie

I don't think I'm the same person anymore. Before Clarissa, I thought I knew all the answers. I knew what was right and what was wrong and everyone should get out of my way. Now I'm not so sure. It's like Clarissa cracked me open, and all this tenderness spilled out of me that I didn't even know I had. But I think it's a good thing. Because without being cracked open, I could never feel the way I do about her. I thought I was strong when I was on my own, but I was really just very heavily guarded. Even though love makes me feel weak, Clarissa and I together are more powerful than anything.

I still think destroying property is the right thing to do, but to be honest I don't feel very motivated to smash capitalism right now. I'm basically a big scaredy-cat. Things that sounded very noble and grand in theory, in real life turned out to be freakin' terrifying. Operating that bulldozer was more frightening than I could have believed. I don't know if I would ever do anything like that again. Maybe I don't have enough righteous anger anymore. My new theme song is "I Am a Poseur" by X-Ray Spex because I think I am one now, but I just don't care. All I do now are bourgeois things like horseback riding and lying around kissing my girlfriend. Is that so wrong?

Clarissa

You know how people say that suffering makes you a better person? Well, that's stupid. I don't believe that for a second. But if someone asked me, Would you rather still be in the Magnificent Manor but not know what you know now and not have Lexie? I would say no, thanks. I prefer to have to share my tiny bedroom in the new apartment with Desi and work two jobs than go back to the way things were before. I can't imagine what my life would be like without Lexie. I'd be so lonely. Who'd make me laugh with her unending bitter commentary? Who'd bore me with movie trivia until I tickle her to make her stop? Who would share Sassy with me and be so crap at riding her? Lexie's parents have calmed down about having me come over, plus they're never home anyway, so we spend most of our time hanging out at her house eating weirdly expensive vegan food. But my favorite times are when we go to the stables together.

Being with Lexie has opened my eyes to the fact that there's more going on in the world than I could ever have imagined. I think she's made me more fierce and brave. Destroying my own house was the most exciting and satisfying thing I ever did. I can't wait to do more things like that.

Love is the most important thing there is. It's bigger than money. It makes you do crazy things. If it wasn't for love, I could never have made it through the worst autumn of my life. But with it, everything was worthwhile.

About the Author

Nora Olsen was born and raised in New York City. She received a B.A. from Brown University. Although her mother, a prize-winning author, warned her not to become a writer, Nora didn't listen. Nora's previous novels are *The End: Five Queer Kids Save the World* and *Swans & Klons*. Her short fiction has appeared in *Collective Fallout* and the anthology *Heiresses of Russ 2011: The Year's Best Lesbian Speculative Fiction*. Nora's goal is to write thrilling stories and novels that LGBTQ teens can see themselves reflected in.

Nora lives in New York's Hudson Valley with her girlfriend, writer Áine Ní Cheallaigh, and their two adorable cats. The highlight of Nora's year is volunteering at Camp Jabberwocky, a summer camp for children and adults with disabilities. Her favorite writing songs are "Shadow Stabbing" by Cake and "Every Day I Write The Book" by Elvis Costello.

Soliloquy Titles From Bold Strokes Books

Frenemy of the People by Nora Olsen. Clarissa and Lexie have despised each other for as long as they can remember, but when they both find themselves helping an unlikely contender for homecoming queen, they are catapulted into an unexpected romance. (978-1-62639-063-8)

The Balance by Neal Wooten. Love and survival come together in the distant future as Piri and Niko faceoff against the worst factions of mankind's evolution. (978-1-62639-055-3)

The Unwanted by Jeffrey Ricker. Jamie Thomas is plunged into danger when he discovers his mother is an Amazon who needs his help to save the tribe from a vengeful god. (978-1-62639-048-5)

Because of Her by KE Payne. When Tabby Morton is forced to move to London, she's convinced her life will never be the same again. But the beautiful and intriguing Eden Palmer is about to show her that this time, change is most definitely for the better. (978-1-62639-049-2)

The Seventh Pleiade by Andrew J. Peters. When Atlantis is besieged by violent storms, tremors, and a barbarian army, it will be up to a young gay prince to find a way for the kingdom's survival. (978-1-60282-960-2)

The Missing Juliet: A Fisher Key Adventure by Sam Cameron. A teenage detective and her friends search for a kidnapped Hollywood star in the Florida Keys. (978-1-60282-959-6)

Asher's Fault by Elizabeth Wheeler. Fourteen-year-old Asher Price sees the world in black and white, much like the photos he takes, but when his little brother drowns at the same moment Asher experiences his first same-sex kiss, he can no longer hide behind the lens of his camera and eventually discovers he isn't the only one with a secret. (978-1-60282-982-4)

Meeting Chance by Jennifer Lavoie. When man's best friend turns on Aaron Cassidy, the teen keeps his distance until fate puts Chance in his hands. (978-1-60282-952-7)

Lake Thirteen by Greg Herren. A visit to an old cemetery seems like fun to a group of five teenagers, who soon learn that sometimes it's best to leave old ghosts alone. (978-1-60282-894-0)

The Road to Her by KE Payne. Sparks fly when actress Holly Croft, star of UK soap *Portobello Road*, meets her new on-screen love interest, the enigmatic and sexy Elise Manford. (978-1-60282-887-2)

Swans and Klons by Nora Olsen. In a future world where there are no males, sixteen-year-old Rubric and her girlfriend Salmon Jo must fight to survive when everything they believed in turns out to be a lie. (978-1-60282-874-2)

Kings of Ruin by Sam Cameron. High school student Danny Kelly and loner Kevin Clark must team up to defeat a top-secret alien intelligence that likes to wreak havoc with fiery car, truck, and train accidents. (978-1-60282-864-3)

Wonderland by David-Matthew Barnes. After her mother's sudden death, Destiny Moore is sent to live with her two gay uncles on Avalon Cove, a mysterious island on which she uncovers a secret place called Wonderland, where love and magic prove to be real. (978-1-60282-788-2)

Another 365 Days by KE Payne. Clemmie Atkins is back, and her life is more complicated than ever! Still madly in love with her girlfriend, Clemmie suddenly finds her life turned upside down with distractions, confessions, and the return of a familiar face... (978-1-60282-775-2)

The Secret of Othello by Sam Cameron. Florida teen detectives Steven and Denny risk their lives to search for a sunken NASA satellite—but under the waves, no one can hear you scream... (978-1-60282-742-4)

Andy Squared by Jennifer Lavoie. Andrew never thought anyone could come between him and his twin sister, Andrea... until Ryder rode into town. (978-1-60282-743-1)

Sara by Greg Herren. A mysterious and beautiful new student at Southern Heights High School stirs things up when students start dying. (978-1-60282-674-8)

Boys of Summer, edited by Steve Berman. Stories of young love and adventure, when the sky's ceiling is a bright blue marvel, when another boy's laughter at the beach can distract from dull summer jobs. (978-1-60282-663-2)

Street Dreams by Tama Wise. Tyson Rua has more than his fair share of problems growing up in New Zealand—he's gay, he's falling in love, and he's run afoul of the local hip-hop crew leader just as he's trying to make it as a graffiti artist. (978-1 60282-650-2)

365 Days by KE Payne. Life sucks when you're seventeen years old and confused about your sexuality, and the girl of your dreams doesn't even know you exist. Then in walks sexy new emo girl, Hannah Harrison. Clemmie Atkins has exactly 365 days to discover herself, and she's going to have a blast doing it! (978-1-60282-540-6)

me@you.com by KE Payne. Is it possible to fall in love with someone you've never met? Imogen Summers thinks so because it's happened to her. (978-1-60282-592-5)

Swimming to Chicago by David-Matthew Barnes. As the lives of the adults around them unravel, high school students Alex and Robby form an unbreakable bond, vowing to do anything to stay together—even if it means leaving everything behind. (978-1-60282-572-7)

Timothy by Greg Herren. *Timothy* is a romantic suspense thriller from award-winning mystery writer Greg Herren set in the fabulous Hamptons. (978-1-60282-760-8)